Praise for

The Dragon Waking

"Thirteen-year-old Rose Gallagher shares only one thing in common with her dad: an interest in rock hunting. When she discovers a rare stone in the Nevada desert, she doesn't expect to find a shape-shifting dragon as well...Jade is the first of her kind to awaken millions of years after the comet that killed the dinosaurs...This fast-paced, imaginative fantasy adventure will appeal to Percy Jackson fans... A strong choice for middle grade fantasy collections."
—*School Library Journal*

The Dragon Waking

GRAYSON TOWLER

ALBERT WHITMAN & COMPANY
CHICAGO, ILLINOIS

Library of Congress Cataloging-in-Publication
data is on file with the publisher.

Printed in the United States of America
10 9 8 7 6 5 4 3 2 1 LB 22 21 20 19 18 17

Design by Jordan Kost

For more information about Albert Whitman & Company,
visit our website at www.albertwhitman.com.

For Candi. Always.

Chapter One

Rose

"That's a dragon!"

Rose's head snapped around at the sound of the voice from behind her.

"She's drawing a dragon!" Trevor Wallace leaned over his desk, pointing over Rose's shoulder at her sketch pad. "Look!" he said, waving his arm. "That's not the assignment!"

"Shut up!" she hissed at him, but she was too late.

Coach Hyatt lumbered across the classroom, angling his bulk between the eighth graders' chairs as he bore down on Rose. He towered over her and stared down at her paper. "What's going on here, Gallagher?"

"I'm just drawing, sir...Coach," Rose said, forcing a smile. She knew he preferred being called "coach," even when he was doing his extra duty as an art teacher.

"That looks to me like a dragon," he said, jabbing a

thick finger at her sketch pad.

Rose looked at her drawing. She couldn't deny it. "Yes, Coach."

Trevor Wallace snickered. Rose shot him a glare that promised painful vengeance.

Rose's friend Lisa spoke up from the seat beside her. "It's really good, though. I bet nobody else drew anything as good."

The picture *was* good. The dragon spread its great bat-like wings across the page, crouching as if preparing to leap aloft. A serpentine tail coiled behind it, and elegant horns curved back from behind its eyes. It was so perfect that it seemed to breathe on the page. The strange thing was that Rose couldn't remember why she'd decided to sketch a dragon. It seemed so familiar, like she'd seen it in a book or a dream. There was no denying it was an excellent drawing, maybe even her best.

This fact did not move Coach Hyatt. "I don't care if it's a dang Picasso! Is it the assignment? *Is* it?" He leaned close to stare into her eyes.

"No, sir," Rose squeaked.

"What was the assignment?" He straightened up and surveyed the class. "Hmm? Anyone remember?"

"Coach!" Trevor's hand shot in the air. "Draw something from our lives, sir!"

"That's right. Now this here"—he knocked a knuckle on Rose's desk—"is make-believe. Did anyone else draw something make-believe? What about you, Wallace?"

Trevor was more than happy to show off. "I drew my baseball glove, Coach."

"Darned right you did," Coach Hyatt said.

Rose made a gagging face at Trevor's pathetic sucking up.

Coach Hyatt whirled and focused on Lisa. "What about you, Miss Sanders? Did you remember the assignment?"

Lisa gave Rose an apologetic look and held up her own sketch pad. "My dog," she said. "It's not very good."

"Good, bad, it doesn't matter!" the coach said. "It's just art. What matters is whether you executed the assignment I gave you. You there! McBee! What did you draw?"

"It's 'just art'?" Lisa whispered as Coach Hyatt heaved himself over to the next desk to continue his inquisition. "What a total goon. I wish Mrs. Jersey taught this class full time instead of just subbing when there's an away game."

Rose could agree with that, but she had another concern. "Do you think he's going around to check on everyone?"

"I think so," Lisa said. "He's on a roll."

Rose still had a chance. She flipped the page in her sketchbook and snatched up her pencil, angling her body so it blocked Trevor's view of what she was doing. If he blabbed again, he'd ruin her plan. Fortunately, Trevor was absorbed in watching the coach stomp around the room and interrogate each student.

"Gomez, let's see," Coach Hyatt said. "A cactus? Good, good. Leeds, what's that supposed to be? Oh, a cat? Looked like a fish. Never mind, good work. Pong, that's a fine-looking car. Your dad's? Good. Now, Ostrom, that's...Wait a minute, Ostrom."

Rose glanced up from her work to see Coach Hyatt towering over the desk of her friend Clay Ostrom. If anyone else had messed up the assignment, it would be Clay. Rose didn't think she'd ever seen Clay draw anything from real life. If it didn't exist in a fantasy epic or a space opera, Clay didn't waste his energy thinking about it.

"That looks like a dinosaur," Coach Hyatt said. "Did you not hear the assignment? Why'd you draw something make-believe, boy?"

"Dinosaurs aren't make-believe!" Clay shot back. He adjusted his glasses and glared up at Coach Hyatt. Clay was skinny and small for a thirteen-year-old, but he wore a ferocious expression of defiance in the face of the looming coach.

Coach Hyatt didn't seem to notice. "Well, there are no dinosaurs in your life, Ostrom. The assignment was..."

"This isn't really a dinosaur," Clay said.

The teacher peered down. "Looks like one to me, boy."

"No, it's a drawing of a *statue* of a dinosaur," Clay said. "See, my uncle works at the Lost World casino down in Vegas, and I go down there all the time to look at their model dinosaurs. This is the statue of a triceratops from the shopping promenade."

The coach's face suddenly lit up with a smile, and he delivered a friendly slap to Clay's back that nearly drove the boy through his desk. "All right, Ostrom! Way to improvise! So, looks like everyone completed the assignment except for you, Gallagher."

Rose sat up at her desk and smiled at him. "But, sir, I did complete it. Look."

Coach Hyatt trundled over to examine Rose's sketch pad. "What's this?"

"It's my horse," she said. "His name's Beans. See?"

As the coach took her pad, Trevor spoke up, his voice ratcheting up to almost a soprano. "But, Coach! She just drew that! The dragon is on the other page!"

This was true. Rose had drawn horses so many times that she could whip up a reasonably good sketch in about a minute. Coach Hyatt's circuit of the class had given her ample time to produce a serviceable illustration of Beans.

A broad grin appeared on the coach's ruddy face. "Now that's how you execute a two-minute drill. Nice hustle, Gallagher!"

"Coach!" Trevor's indignant squeak sent ripples of giggles through the classroom.

"Pipe down, you hamburger heads!" Coach Hyatt commanded over the babble. "I've got homework for you." Rose listened as he rattled off the assignment, smiling in satisfaction as Trevor Wallace muttered angrily behind her. When the bell sounded, she lingered to pack her backpack while her classmates crowded toward the door, eager to be on their way home.

"Can I look at it?"

Rose turned to see Clay threading his way awkwardly through the other students. She gave him a curious look. "At what?"

"The dragon," he said. "Can I see it?"

"Oh. Sure."

Clay flipped aside the page with her impromptu horse drawing, his eyes widening as they lit upon the dragon. "Wow. That's awesome," he said, his voice tinged with a mixture of respect and envy. She knew he was only a passable artist himself, no matter how much he practiced. "That's your best yet."

"You think?"

Clay had seen plenty of her drawings over the years and had even hung some of her pictures of knights and monsters on his bedroom wall. He never held back his criticism when she missed some detail on a suit of medieval plate mail or if she got the heads on a chimera wrong, so his admiration meant a lot.

"Easily," he said. "Where'd you get the idea?"

"I'm not sure," she said. The dragon had just burst onto the page. Sometimes drawing was like that for her, but this time she'd really lost herself in her art.

"It's so good." He tapped the sketch pad. "You should frame it. See you later, Rose."

"Frame it," she said, looking at the drawing. Yes, she could frame it and hang it up. Her dad might even agree to spring for a nice frame if she asked. But only if she asked. She still remembered a time years ago when her mother had plastered the walls with Rose's drawings, lovingly displaying the most colorful ones in bright cardboard frames.

After her mother died when Rose was six, it fell to

Rose to decide if any of her art should go on the fridge or the walls. Her father never discouraged her...but he never offered to help. She wondered if he would even recognize that this drawing was her best work.

Lost in her thoughts, Rose didn't notice Trevor edging her way until it was too late. Suddenly, a splash of something sticky and cold struck her on the side of the head. She jumped in surprise and caught her foot on her chair leg. Rose let out a startled yelp as she tumbled to the floor, thick fluid covering one side of her head. Trevor stood over her, holding a dripping canister of white paint, now mostly empty.

"Oops!" Trevor said, his voice full of artificial concern. "Sorry, Gallagher! I tripped."

Rose ran her fingers through her hair and came away with a thick smear of white paint on her hand. Rage sizzled to life in her blood. "You little *turd!*"

Before she could get to her feet, Trevor bolted for the door, trailing a whooping laugh behind him. Rose looked around for Coach Hyatt, but he'd already left the classroom, eager to get down to the field for after-school soccer practice. She picked herself up off the floor, peering at her shoulder to check the damage.

When she looked down at her sketch pad, she saw a white blotch on her dragon drawing, its delicate pencil lines smeared away in the paint. Rose stared at it in disbelief for several seconds, and then a shout of outrage burst from her throat.

"I'm going to *kill* him!"

She might have actually launched herself in pursuit of Trevor, but Lisa was suddenly there at her side, snatching a handful of paper towels from the art supply table and going to work on the mess. "Ugh," her friend said. "It's all over your shirt and hair. Come over to the sink."

"Look what he did to my drawing!"

Lisa looked at the sketch pad and let out a moan. "Rose! You should report him."

"I should wring his stupid neck."

Lisa steered the fuming Rose to the sink and cleaned her up in earnest. "It's coming off your skin okay, though you've got a skunk streak in your bangs."

"Stylish."

"Very."

Her hair felt stiff on the left side, but she thought it would come out in the shower. "I need to cool off before I get home," she said. "Do you want to go rock hunting with me?"

Lisa rolled her eyes. "Only *you* would 'cool off' by hiking around the desert."

"Wanna come?"

"Can't," Lisa said. "Piano lessons. Find something shiny out there for me, okay?"

"Maybe I'll get lucky," Rose said, looking down at the smeared remnants of the dragon on her sketch pad. She'd have to discover something pretty incredible to make up for what a rotten day this had been so far.

* * *

Rose stomped across the desert sand, trying to forget that idiot Trevor Wallace. This was the first time he'd destroyed something she cared about with one of his stupid pranks. She could probably report him and get him in trouble, but that sort of retaliation felt unworthy somehow. Rose liked to handle her own problems, not go whining to the authorities every time someone rubbed her the wrong way. She picked up her pace, pushing herself to force thoughts of Trevor out of her head.

The desert welcomed her like an old friend, inviting her along a familiar narrow footpath that wound between jutting stones and dry clumps of sage. The faint scent of creosote in the air soothed her angry nerves. Rose loved to venture out in the desert, whether on foot or on horseback. Somehow, even when she came by herself, she never felt alone.

This afternoon she pursued her ongoing quest to uncover interesting stones. Most of her classmates couldn't tell a chunk of worthless basalt from a nugget of Nevada lapis, but Rose had been trained in the secrets of stones all her life, peering over the tabletop as her father sorted through piles of rocks to feed into his noisy tumbler for polishing.

Today, she was looking for geodes—mottled eggs of limestone that looked utterly mundane on the outside, but revealed glittering crystalline caves within when they were cracked open. These were her favorite.

She knew she had a particularly good chance of making a find that day. A rare rainstorm had cast its fury down onto the desert earlier that month. During such a deluge, the parched earth became saturated quickly until it turned into water-repellent clay. Such storms led to flash floods that swept across the dry riverbeds, kicking up debris and rapidly eroding large chunks of sand. The upside to these floods was that sometimes they unearthed buried deposits of stone, creating a perfect opportunity for a rockhound like Rose to find something special.

She hoped so. It would be good to have something to bring back to her father. A love of stones was one of the few things they still shared.

Unfortunately, flash floods turned up garbage as well as treasure. As she reached the lip of a new trench that the floodwaters had carved across the familiar landscape, Rose saw a twisted stack of metal and plastic half buried in the sand. An uprooted Joshua tree lay tangled with the remains of an old dirt bike that had been battered and broken by the chaotic forces of the torrent. She wondered if the rushing waters had claimed a portion of someone's backyard where the motorcycle had been stored.

Rose spotted one end of the handlebar that had broken off at the base. What remained was a bar the perfect length to serve as a sword. She picked it up, tested its weight, and brandished it at the sky. "Who dares to challenge me?" she called out.

When she'd played fantasy games with Clay, he always liked to play the sorcerer, while she took the role of a knight or a warrior. She flourished her weapon as if for the benefit of an unseen audience, then whirled and faced the uprooted Joshua tree. "I see you there, villain!" she cried, picturing Trevor Wallace's face superimposed over the squashed bristles of the plant. "Trying to ambush me, eh? Have at you!"

Rose launched herself at the Joshua tree, putting all her weight into an overhand swing. The impact of aluminum on wood sent a satisfying shock down her arm. "Take that, art ruiner!" She rained down more blows, punctuating each with an insult. "Hair puller! Mouth breather! Fart lighter!"

This felt so good that she soon adopted more targets. The deflated front tire of the bike became Coach Hyatt. "You call yourself a teacher? Receive your punishment, you lard sandwich!" Her weapon flashed, vanquishing imagined phantoms with each strike.

Finally, she stepped back from the battlefield and raised her sword. "I have conquered. All hail Warrior Princess Rose! The treasure is mine by rights."

A green gleam caught her eye.

Rose focused on the glint of sunlight from a reflective surface. There was something beneath the spiny fingers of a yucca. She dropped the handlebar and moved in for a closer look. It was a large teardrop-shaped stone about the size of her fist. It caught the sunlight so brilliantly that it appeared to glow with its own inner radiance.

She stared at the stone with wonder. It was unlike anything she'd ever seen. A thrill surged through her as her fingers brushed the glassy surface. The translucent stone was surprisingly heavy—much denser than regular glass. Tiny, delicate ripples crisscrossed its surface, creating a sparkling dance of light.

Rose knew all the local rocks quite well. Trained from childhood by her father and grandfather, she could identify every kind of mineral that southern Nevada had to offer. This stone wasn't from around here. It shouldn't have been here at all.

"It's a tektite," she whispered. "Has to be."

Rose remembered her father teaching her about tektites. They formed when a really massive meteor hit the earth with an impact big enough to kick chunks of molten debris thousands of feet up into the freezing stratosphere. When the crystallized remnants fell back to earth, they landed as tektites. She'd seen pictures of tektites and even some black ones in person at a gem show in Las Vegas a couple years before. Those tiny, black blobs were nothing compared to the wonder she now held.

"But there are only a few places in the world where you find tektites," she said, peering into the depths of the gold-green stone. "And Nevada isn't one of them. So what are you doing here, hmm?"

Rose held the stone close to her face, studying the minute golden flecks suspended within the green translucence. This had to be the greatest thing she'd ever found. Her mind began to race with the possibilities.

She'd be published in scientific journals, applauded for her amazing discovery.

How much was the stone worth? But the thought of selling it suddenly wrenched her heart. She didn't want it to go into a museum. She wanted to keep it and stare into it forever, to let herself fall into the strange world hidden within the stone's green and gold beauty...

A loud noise shocked her out of her daydreams of glory as something *heavy* thumped onto the ground nearby.

Rose whirled around, almost dropping the tektite. She gripped the strap on her backpack, her eyes widening as she listened.

Something made a low, rumbling sound. Not an engine. Something alive.

The noise emanated from around the curve of the flood bed, its source concealed by an eroded ridge of sand and dirt. Rose saw a plume of dust puff into the air above the lip of the trench, and she heard the twigs of a dried-out tumbleweed snapping. Something let out a heavy snort.

"Hello?" she called. Her voice came out in a strangled squeak.

The rumbling stopped instantly. Had it heard her?

Rose swallowed hard, her heart beating fast as she

tried to figure out what could have made such a noise. A horse taking a really bad fall might do it. Maybe a rider had come out this way, or an escaped horse was wandering alone.

And they might be hurt. That thumping sound hadn't been good.

She had to check it out. Rose dropped the tektite into her backpack, then edged forward, her feet sinking into the fine silt of the flood bed. If the horse was scared, she'd have to be especially calm for both of them.

Rose rounded the bend and looked down the path carved by the flash flood.

A dragon looked back at her.

Chapter Two

Jade

For a moment, Rose couldn't move. Her whole body clenched like an overwound spring, her breath freezing in her throat. The sight of the vast creature filled her eyes and paralyzed her thoughts. Sunlight gleamed off green scales and enormous translucent wings that cast their shadow along the dry riverbed. It was a dragon, as solid as the stones and creosote bushes, standing there in stark defiance of everything Rose knew to be true.

The dragon parted its jaws slightly, exposing teeth like pearl-white daggers, and let out a chuffing breath. Rose stared transfixed into eyes like living emeralds.

Then the creature took a step toward her, and Rose whirled and ran.

She heard a rumbling grunt as loud as a semitruck, then the thud of heavy footsteps. Rose screamed and sprinted as fast as her legs could carry her, the soft sand sucking at her boots and slowing her down. She pelted past the wrecked motorcycle and threw herself at the slope of the dry flood bed, gouging out handfuls of sand as she scrambled up the grade. She hauled herself out of the trench and took off across the desert.

Something crunched behind her, and she dared a look back. The dragon loomed out of the sandy trench and examined something stuck to its front claws. It had stepped on the dirt bike. It gave its foreleg a mighty shake, and the debris flew free. Then it swiveled its great head on its sinewy neck and focused on Rose again.

A terrified whimper emerged from her throat.

The dragon lunged up the steep side of the flood bed, but the loose sand gave way under its great bulk. The creature tumbled over backward with a startled bugling sound, kicking up massive clouds of sand and dust as it collapsed in the miniature avalanche.

Rose tore her eyes away from the spectacle. A rocky cliff face climbed out of the sand no more than a hundred yards away—she might find some place she could hide there. She dropped her backpack and ran for all she was worth.

Something behind her made a tremendous *whooshing* sound. She risked a quick look over her shoulder and saw a swirling trail of dust rising from the flood bed into the sky. A massive winged shadow slid across the desert.

A part of her mind gibbered that this was impossible, completely impossible. It had to be a dream! A nightmare! But that didn't matter, because everything else in her howled to run away from the creature. Fiery pain burned in her lungs, and her legs ached in protest as she pushed them harder than she ever had, desperate to reach shelter before the winged monster swooped down and took her in its claws.

The shadow expanded as the dragon descended. Rose heard a quick snapping of wind blowing across the taut membrane of the creature's wings. She shrieked and covered her head. Useless, she knew. The creature could snatch her up whole in one bite. But no attack came. The dragon's vast shadow passed over her again.

Rose threw herself the last few yards toward a space between two large boulders at the base of the rocky slope. She squirmed her way in, praying that the space would be too narrow for the beast to reach.

What if it could breathe fire?

Frantic and sweating, she wedged herself into the space as far as she could. Then she froze, waiting. Rose stared back through the narrow space, able to see only a slice of the desert beyond.

For a long moment, the only sounds were of her rapid-tempo breaths.

Then a plume of sand puffed up, and she heard the beating of the immense wings. The thump of the landing dragon sent a pulse of vibration through her hiking boots. Rose let out a trembling moan as one massive eye peered through the little crevice at her. The dragon studied her for several seconds, then pulled its head back and reached into the crack with one claw.

Her shelter wasn't good enough. The great talon loomed closer.

"No!" Rose screamed.

The claw jerked to a stop, then withdrew.

Rose stared in astonishment. The dragon peered at her once again, then backed off a few steps. It sat back on its haunches and regarded her with those extraordinary eyes, cocking its head slightly back and forth, making soft muttering noises to itself.

It wasn't attacking.

The dragon could have easily plucked her out of the inadequate hiding place. And she knew it could have caught her long before she got to the rocks if it had wanted. So why had it chased her?

The dragon shifted its great bulk and Rose felt her throat clench, but the creature didn't come any closer.

Instead, it hunkered down—folding its wings tight against its back and wrapping its tail around its legs—and rested its chin delicately on its front claws.

The dragon didn't move, except to occasionally flick the end of its tail. For several long moments, Rose and the dragon stared at each other in the silent desert.

Rose felt her breathing begin to slow to a calmer pace. She shifted her position to relieve the pressure from a sharp rock in her back. The dragon twitched but seemed to deliberately settle back into its waiting pose. It was, she realized, making itself as small and nonthreatening as a creature its size could be.

That wasn't the way a predator or a hunter would act.

"Hello?" she called out. Her voice emerged muffled and squeaky.

The elegant spiny ruff that framed the dragon's face perked up with curiosity at the sound of Rose's voice. The dragon let out a soft little chirp.

Rose swallowed her fear, increasingly sure that the dragon meant her no harm. She wriggled herself free from her stony hiding place and hauled herself out of the crack into the open air.

The dragon raised its head very slightly, watching her intently.

Rose still trembled at the sight of the dragon's long

talons and massive jaws, but she mustered her courage and edged closer. The dragon slowly extended its great head toward her as she approached, a posture that suggested both restraint and intense curiosity.

Rose's sense of fear melted into wonder. Never had she seen anything lovelier than the tremendous green dragon before her. The elegant shape of its head and neck, the subtle shadings of green on each of its diamond-shaped scales, the delicate patterns on the translucent membranes of its folded wings— every feature of the dragon struck a perfect balance between beauty and power.

Once again, some part of her insisted that she was dreaming. "Are...are you real?" she asked the impossible creature.

Though the dragon didn't offer an answer, it moved its head closer to gently sniff the air. Rose could make out the scent of its warm breath, tangy and smoky. If this was a dream, it was hands-down the most mind-blowingly vivid one she'd ever had.

The dragon's face hovered just a foot or so in front of her. Rose reached out slowly, tentatively, and rested her hand on the smooth scales of its muzzle.

She had a moment of feeling the unexpected warmth and pliancy of the scales beneath her fingers before her vision went swimmy, as if her eyes were full of the shimmering waves of distortion that arose from hot sand. She thought she might be fainting and struggled to keep a grip on her consciousness.

Then the world righted itself, and the dragon was gone. In its place stood a human girl.

Rose had the impression of looking into a fun-house mirror that turned everything just a little different and shifted most of the colors to green. The girl before her wore an outfit of overalls and a T-shirt almost identical to Rose's, except every article appeared in shades of green, right down to the braided leather bracelets she'd made herself.

She could have been Rose's cousin—she looked the same age and of a similar build, though paler and without Rose's freckles. Instead of Rose's red hair, the stranger's was the deep color of pine needles with an odd streak of green so light it was nearly white running along the left side of her head.

Rose squeezed her eyes shut and shook her head. This day just kept getting weirder.

"What's going on here?" she asked.

The green-haired girl said nothing as she blinked around at her surroundings, wearing a mingled look of surprise and delight. She examined her hands, opening and closing the fingers in deliberate motions, then ran her fingers across her hair. The girl let out a laugh, then put her hands to her mouth as if surprised by the sound of her own voice.

"Hey," Rose said. "Um...are you okay?"

The girl looked at her.

"Can you understand me?" Rose asked.

Rose saw interest in those brilliant-green eyes, but no sign of comprehension. The stranger took a step forward and stumbled, coming down awkwardly. Instinctively, Rose lunged to her aid and caught her before she fell. A strange tingle passed through Rose as she touched the dragon-girl, like the hum of an electric current.

The girl grasped Rose by the arm and let herself be guided back to balance.

Clearly the green-haired girl wasn't used to her new body. "Come on," Rose said. "Here. This is how you walk." With that, she led the girl slowly along with careful steps. The stranger picked up the knack of walking within just a few paces and soon found her equilibrium. She let go of Rose's supporting arms and took a few steps on her own, then suddenly did a clumsy spin and nearly lost her balance again, laughing as Rose caught her.

"You imitated how I look," Rose said. She didn't know how this could possibly be true, but the whole situation was already completely unreal. Another flash of insight came to her. "You had to touch me first," she said. "That's why you chased me."

The girl said nothing and kept smiling. Did she understand anything?

"You're not stuck this way, are you?" Rose asked. "Could you turn back if you wanted? I read a story about a unicorn that got turned into a human and couldn't change back." Rose curled her fingers into claws and spread her arms, trying to make herself look bigger. "You changed yourself, right? So you can change back." She added to her pantomime by making a flapping motion with her arms. "If you wanted, you could..."

Suddenly she felt that swimmy sensation again, and the dragon burst into view before her in all its glory. A gust of wind blew back the hair from Rose's face as the dragon spread her translucent wings wide enough to block out the horizon. Rose let out a startled squeak and stumbled in retreat, tripping and falling on her butt.

Rose's heartbeat took off to a gallop, but this time it wasn't from fear. She found herself gripped with a longing to experience the thrill of being carried skyward on those enormous wings, to feel them driving her into the sky with each swooping beat. She wondered what it would be like to grab on to the dragon's neck and ride her aloft, faster than any horse, the ground shrinking away as they hurtled together into the sky...

The world shimmered once more, and the dragon became a human girl again and looked down at Rose with concern.

With a weak laugh, Rose got to her feet. The vision of flying with the dragon had left her strangely breathless. "You're...you're *real*," she whispered. "You're really real." She let out a shaky laugh. "How is this possible?"

The girl's brow furrowed as she stared intently at Rose. She seemed to be trying to understand, but Rose wasn't sure if she grasped the meaning of speech.

Rose decided to try something simple. She pointed to herself, exaggerating the gesture. "Rose," she said, then repeated it.

The green-eyed girl considered this for a long moment. Finally she took a swallow and spoke her first word: "Rose." The name floated in the air like a snatch of song.

"Good!" An elated grin bloomed onto Rose's face, mirrored by the dragon-girl. "Can you tell me your name?" She pointed to herself, said her own name again, then pointed to the other girl and waited.

The girl grasped her intention almost immediately. She pointed to herself in a precise imitation of Rose's own gesture, and then opened her mouth. What emerged was something between a screech and a growl loud enough to make Rose jump.

The girl's eyes widened in shock, and she poked curiously at her throat and mouth.

Rose laughed. "Wow. That's...quite a name! It probably sounds better when you say it as a dragon, huh?"

A puzzled look was the only response she got.

"Look," Rose said, "I need to be able to call you something. Is it okay if I come up with a name?"

A tiny smile flitted across the green-eyed girl's face.

"I'll take that as a yes," Rose said. The stories she knew about dragons didn't give her much to go on—she didn't think anything like Tiamat or Smaug was going to work. She thought through her mental catalog of green rocks and gemstones. "Let's see...emerald? No, that's not a name. Variscite is a pretty stone, but...no. Not so good."

The other girl listened, a look of lively interest on her face.

"Okay, there's olivine. That's green. Maybe shortened to Olive? No, wait, there's an Olive Dunsdale down the block, and she's a drama queen." Rose rubbed the bridge of her nose and closed her eyes. "There's got to be something."

Rose examined the girl again, letting her eyes linger on the colors in her hair, and suddenly a name came to her in a flash.

"Jade!" she said, and she knew it was right.

The dragon-girl's eyes widened.

Rose pointed at her. "Jade."

"Jade," the girl repeated, tapping herself on the chest.

Rose grinned at her new friend. "So we've got a name for you!"

Jade giggled. Rose laughed along with her, a giddy sensation of euphoria flooding her mind. She didn't know how a creature out of legend had found its way into her life. It was real, not a dream, yet it was also impossible—and utterly wonderful. The last remnants of her initial fear unwound and spooled into joy throughout her body. Jade clasped her hand and they laughed together, their voices mingling across the sun-baked waste.

Their laughter finally exhausted itself and tapered off slowly to silence.

"So," Rose asked. "What happens now?"

Jade said nothing but looked at her with an expectant smile.

"I guess we'll figure it out," Rose said.

Chapter Three

A Strange and Dangerous Guest

By the time Rose made it to the sanctuary of her home, she was covered in sweat and breathing like she'd run a marathon. She closed the front door behind her and slumped against the wood, panting hard.

Jade, who didn't seem the least bit tired or affected by the Nevada heat, cocked her head and gave Rose a look of both curiosity and concern. "Rose?" she said.

"I'm okay," Rose gasped. "We're home. It's all good."

The dragon-girl smiled and began to stare in avid fascination around the kitchen.

Rose shook her head in exhausted bewilderment. Jade might be a dragon, but she had the reckless curiosity of a kitten. Everything she encountered was a new source of wonder for the strange girl—and she had to touch it all. Rose had spent the entire journey home herding Jade away from danger, keeping her from touching a wickedly spined cactus or walking headlong in front of a moving delivery truck. She seemed completely oblivious to the idea that anything could be a threat to her.

Now she had to figure out what to do with a dragon. There was no way she could hope to pass Jade off as a normal girl. She might look human, but she clearly didn't know how to act like one.

And why was she here, anyway?

Rose couldn't wrap her mind around the scope of what Jade meant in her life. In one moment, everything she'd believed about what was true had flipped on its head. Her father, her teachers, and all the adults in her life were fundamentally wrong about what was possible in the world. The implications left her feeling dizzy.

And Jade wasn't providing any answers. She'd picked up a few words, like her name, but they were nowhere near meaningful communication.

"It's really hard not to be able to talk to you, Jade."

"Jade," agreed the girl.

Rose sighed, then flicked on the switch to the overhead light.

Jade gave a little jump of surprise and then gasped in delight. She reached over and flipped the switch the other way, and the lights went dark. The dragon-girl laughed.

"Look, could we..."

Jade flipped the switch up, then down, then up again.

"Why don't we..."

Jade flicked the light switch quickly from on to off, causing the lights to strobe.

"Jade! Stop!"

Her new friend gave her a puzzled look but released the switch. She tucked her hands behind her back and grinned.

"You are so *weird*. I mean, you're a dragon, and you can change shape...and you get all jazzed about a light switch? I don't get you at all."

"Weird," Jade said.

"Yeah, weird." Rose ran her fingers through her hair and immediately felt the stiff patch where Trevor Wallace's paint attack had landed. "Yuck. I feel so gross. Come on. You can wait in my room while I clean up."

Rose led the way through the house, their pace slowed by Jade's haphazard interest in the things she saw on the way. It was strange what seemed to capture her curiosity. Rose's father's colorful collection of rare stones barely registered, but Jade marveled at the seam where the wall and ceiling came together. She stopped to examine a quilt, peering closely as she traced the delicate lines of the stitching with a finger. Rose pulled her gently away, steering her toward her room.

"Now, stay in here for a couple minutes," she said. "I just have to...Oh, not *again!*"

Jade flicked the light switch on and off several times, watching the reaction from Rose's lamp with a look of satisfaction.

"Fine, fine. Knock yourself out. I'll be back in a minute." She grabbed her bathrobe off its hook and hastily pulled a new shirt and shorts out of her closet. The lights stopped flickering, and Rose turned to see Jade studying her curiously. "What?"

The dragon-girl gave no answer.

"Look, just play with the switch for a while," she said. She held up one hand, palm out, in what she hoped was a clear gesture. "Stay. Do you understand? Stay."

"Stay," Jade repeated.

It would have to do. Rose slipped out the door, closing it behind her quickly so Jade wouldn't follow. Her mind raced as she headed for the shower. What could she possibly say to her dad? She thought about telling him that she'd made a new friend, and could she possibly stay over, at least until she figures out not to run into traffic by herself? Oh, and she's really a dragon, by the way. True story.

Heck, her dad wouldn't be able to deal with Rose having a friend with green hair, much less one who was a magical creature.

Rose mulled this over as she climbed into the shower, letting cool water rush over her and wash away the grime and sweat. What, really, did she know about dragons? Or more to the point, how much of what she thought she knew about dragons was the truth? Just a few hours ago, she would've said anything about dragons was just make-believe, so the idea that there even was a "truth" to consider took a lot of getting used to.

Jade had wings, so she could probably fly. Could she breathe fire? That seemed to be a common trait in most of the stories, but there was no telling how far fantasy literature and movies could be trusted to guide her. Rose certainly didn't remember anything about dragons being able to turn into people.

In most of the stories, dragons were selfish and greedy. Jade didn't seem to be either. They gathered big piles of gold and sat on them in caves, devoured maidens, and ravaged countrysides—none of which seemed like the sort of thing Jade was interested in. Other books depicted friendly dragons that let people ride them, dragons that could read minds, dragons that fought side by side with people against evil despots or deadly monsters...but all those stories were told about places long ago or worlds that had never existed. What was she supposed to do with a dragon that had popped up a few miles away from her house and then came home and played with her light switches?

Rose vigorously scrubbed shampoo into her hair, as if her fingers could dig answers out through her scalp. Suddenly, the shower curtain swished aside, and Jade stood there, staring at her with wide eyes.

Rose let out a little shriek and yanked the curtain back to cover herself. "Hey!"

"Hey!" Jade mimicked.

"Look...Give me a little privacy, okay?" Rose flailed her hand toward the door. "Go! I'll be right out. Okay? Go back to my room, Jade!"

All her pointing and shouting must've done the trick, because Jade turned and wandered away, pausing a moment to turn the lights on and off a few times before she eventually left the bathroom. Rose rinsed her hair in a hurry, worried about what other trouble Jade might get into if left alone.

But Jade was still in Rose's room a few minutes later, much to Rose's relief. As Rose was pulling on her shoes, she realized something had changed about the dragon-girl. "Hey, why are you wearing my clothes?"

Jade sat on Rose's bed, now dressed in a completely new outfit. She had discarded her green clothing from the desert and had confiscated a T-shirt, shorts, and some slip-on shoes from Rose's closet.

"What's the matter with the clothes you had...um?" She looked around, but saw no sign of the green outfit that Jade had been wearing in the desert. Rose checked the closet, looked under the bed, and even peered out the door to see if the dragon-girl had dropped her clothes in the hall on the way from the bathroom. She turned back to Jade, puzzled. "What happened to your...Oh. Oh!"

Realization hit her, and Rose felt her face reddening. Jade hadn't been *wearing* clothes before. Dragons probably didn't know what they even were. She'd imitated Rose's appearance but had assumed that the clothing was part of her body until she learned otherwise. "I took you all the way through town naked," Rose said, then let out an embarrassed giggle.

Jade probably didn't understand, but she laughed along with Rose anyway.

She was good-natured at least. And she looked more normal in Rose's clothes. "All right, here's what we'll do," Rose said. "I'll tell Dad that you're new in town and you don't speak much English." That wouldn't be a lie, technically speaking. "He'll think you're an oddball, but that's okay. I think he'll be cool with you staying over for tonight."

As plans went, it wasn't much. Hopefully her father would be tired after work, as he often was, and wouldn't ask too many questions about where Jade came from or how long she was going to be here.

At best, that plan would only work for one night. Then she'd be back where she started.

The only thing Rose could think of was to go through her mother's old books. Her mom had loved folklore and mythology and had kept a collection of books filled with stories and pictures of fantastic beasts. Rose had loved reading these with her mother, even if sometimes the stories were scary. She remembered one about a dragon—the legend of the greedy Fafnir and the hero Sigurd who killed the creature and learned to speak the language of all living things after tasting the dragon's blood. Maybe there would be something in those books that could give her a hint about what Jade was doing here.

"And then what?" she asked aloud, mostly to herself. She had no idea. Nothing in her life had prepared her for the sudden appearance of a cheerful, inquisitive dragon who seemed to want nothing more than to mess with everything she could get her hands on.

Jade paused in her inspection of the various knick-knacks and souvenirs Rose kept on her dresser, her attention zeroing in on one small object. The dragon-girl snatched the thing that had caught her interest, then held out her discovery. In her palm she held a small plastic dinosaur. Rose recognized it as the three-horned triceratops.

"You like that?" Rose asked. "I got it from Clay." It was one of the countless souvenirs he'd gotten from the prehistoric-themed Lost World casino.

Jade scrutinized the little figurine, running her fingers over every inch of its molded surface. She turned it back and forth, her eyebrows drawing together in concentration.

"Something wrong?" Rose asked.

The air around Jade's hand began to shimmer. Rose had seen this phenomenon when Jade changed her shape. Out in the desert, it had looked like a heat mirage rising off the baking sand. Here in her room, it felt more like something happening in her own head, like her eyes couldn't focus properly on what she was seeing. Rose reached out and grabbed the side of the dresser for support, feeling dizzy.

The figurine began to change.

Colors shifted and swam along the flanks of the small triceratops. The faded paint of the figurine deepened and became a vivid pattern of deep walnut-colored spots on a reddish-brown field. The texture of the plastic body flowed, the simple details sharpening to lifelike realism. Jade's smile widened. Her eyes seemed to glow with some inner luminescence, and the air pulsed in nearly invisible waves around her hand.

The plastic eyes of the triceratops gleamed like drops of oil. The little figurine began to move, pawing Jade's palm with a white-tipped foot, opening its mouth as if to roar, raising its tiny horns as if to challenge an unseen enemy. Rose gaped in wonder.

Then she heard the doorbell chime.

"Crap!" Rose jumped at the sound, accidentally hitting Jade's extended hand. The little figurine toppled to the floor, and the shimmering in the air ceased as Jade's enchantment broke. Rose picked the figurine up. All the details Jade had added were still there, but the dinosaur no longer moved as if alive.

The doorbell sounded again. "Stay here," Rose told Jade, then headed to the front door.

Clay Ostrom stood on the landing, a plastic shopping bag in his hand. "Hey, Rose."

"Oh. Clay. What's up?"

"I came by to...Hey, who's that?" He peered over her shoulder.

Jade had evidently decided not to stay meekly in the bedroom. There was nothing for Rose to do but brazen it out. "This is my friend Jade," Rose said. "She doesn't speak much English. She's...Dutch." It was the first thing that popped into her head.

"Dutch? Really?" Clay stared in open fascination. "Awesome hair."

"It's all the rage in Europe," Rose lied breezily. "So what's up?" She hoped she could get him to go away. Clay was a friend, but she didn't know if she should let anybody know about Jade, and keeping the secret would be hard if the dragon-girl started doing more magic in front of other people.

"I'm here about the dragon," Clay said.

"*What?*"

Clay took a surprised step back. "Jeez, what's your deal? I had this frame around, and I thought it would be the right size for your drawing."

"Oh!" Rose put a hand to her chest. "Oh. My drawing. Right. It got ruined."

Clay couldn't have looked more aghast if she'd told him she had a terminal illness. "How? What happened?"

She rolled her eyes, feeling a residual surge of her

earlier anger. "Trevor Wallace, the idiot. He dumped paint all over me, and it splashed on my sketch pad."

"That...that...What a tool!" Clay spluttered, every bit as enraged as Rose had been. "That's just *wrong*! Did you tell Mr. Hyatt?"

"No." She doubted that Coach "It's Just Art" Hyatt would've cared.

"Well, you should," Clay said. "That was a masterpiece, Rose. You should tell the principal. Wallace should be—"

"I should be what, geek-wad?" came Trevor Wallace's voice.

Rose gritted her teeth in exasperation and turned to see Trevor and his two goonish friends, Ted and Roger, emerging from the open garage next door. Ted was her next-door neighbor. It would just figure that he and his friends would be hanging out at his place today. The three boys swaggered into her yard, wearing their typical smug expressions.

"Hey, who's she?" Ted pointed at Jade.

"She's a friend," Rose said. "She doesn't speak English. She's Dutch."

"Oh," Roger said. "A Swiss miss! Got any hot chocolate?"

"The Dutch aren't from Switzerland, you idiot," Rose said.

"She's not wearing wooden shoes," Ted said, pointing at Jade's feet.

"What do you call that hair?" Roger asked with a snort. "Green skunk style?"

The trio shared a round of mocking laughter. Rose looked around at Jade, wondering how she would react to this. The dragon-girl regarded the boys with an unsettlingly blank expression, not at all like the inquisitive look she normally wore.

Clay was still glaring at the trio with undisguised anger, and Trevor finally took notice. "What's your problem, Ostrom? Still mad I spilled paint on your girlfriend's scribble?"

Any one of these boys could've beaten Clay up with one hand. He still faced them with a bubbling, righteous fury. "You should be expelled," he said. "Or at least kicked off the basketball team."

That threat wiped the smile off Trevor's face. Expulsion didn't seem likely, but a bullying charge spoken to the principal might very well get Trevor suspended from competing in sports. He advanced on Clay, scowling down at the smaller boy. "You better keep your trap shut, Ostrom."

With more courage than caution, Clay said, "Or what?"

Trevor's hand shot out, and he grabbed Clay's skinny arm. Rose could see Trevor's fingers digging in deep. "Are you going to keep your mouth shut, punk?" he snarled.

"Let go!" Clay struggled uselessly, his defiant expression transforming into pain.

"Get your hands off him!" Rose shouted.

Trevor ignored her and gave Clay a bone-rattling shake. "Well, pip-squeak?"

Rose's anger boiled inside her at Trevor's abuse of a smaller victim. It made her so furious that she felt almost dizzy, like her vision was starting to swim...

Then she realized it wasn't dizziness at all. The air had begun to shimmer.

Her rage changed into panic in a heartbeat. She turned and saw Jade glaring down on the scene from the top of the landing, her green eyes blazing with an unearthly light. Fury radiated from her like heat, yet it made her somehow both beautiful and terrible. The pulsing waves of her power distorted the atmosphere in a rapidly quickening rhythm.

None of the boys noticed. They were focused on Trevor and Clay.

Rose understood with sudden, horrifying clarity. Jade was about to turn back into a dragon. What would

Jade do? Did she see Trevor as a threat? Would she actually attack a bunch of foolish, helpless teenagers...

"Jade, *no!*" Rose screamed. She rushed to her friend and grabbed her by the arms as hard as she could. "*Stop! Stop!*"

The air stilled. The inner radiance faded from Jade's eyes. "Rose?" she said, giving her a questioning look.

Trevor actually let go of Clay in surprise. Rose's cry had been full of real terror, and it had cut through the atmosphere like an edge of broken glass. They all stood frozen, uncertain, staring at the two girls with something between confusion and fear.

Rose turned and shouted at them, her voice hoarse. "You're scaring her! She's not from here, okay? She doesn't understand any of this."

Trevor was the first to recover. "Don't get your undies in a bunch, Gallagher. Me and Ostrom are just having a little man-to-man chat."

"Shut your face!" Rose stormed down the short flight of stairs, her body trembling with a mixture of fear and rage. Trevor took a surprised step back, eyes widening.

"Hey, back off..." he said.

"You're no 'man,' Trevor Wallace." Rose kept advancing, glaring into Trevor's startled face. "You're a bully and a creep, and you make me sick."

She knew instinctively that she had to get rid of these idiots—and fast. If Jade saw them as a threat, she might roast them where they stood. Rose's heart hammered as she advanced. If it came to a real fight, she'd be in trouble. But it was just like dealing with horses...she'd learned to make them *think* she was bigger and stronger than they were. That meant showing no fear, even when she felt scared. Rose pressed forward, driving all three of the boys back with her voice and her will.

"Nobody's going to tattle on you, Trevor," she said. "It was my drawing you ruined, and I'm not squealing to anybody about it."

"Hey, okay," Trevor said. "But what about—"

"Clay!" Rose kept her eyes locked on Trevor's as she called to her friend. "Go home, okay? We'll talk later."

"Oh...okay, Rose," Clay said. "Uh...See you."

She heard his footsteps on the sidewalk as he pelted away but did not turn to look. Trevor stayed pinned under her gaze, his bravado replaced by squirming uncertainty. "There. You're safe, Trevor. Happy? Good. Then get off my property."

With obvious relief, Trevor and his friends scrambled back to the safety of Ted's driveway. They were already snickering at each other, trying to make a big joke of the fact that they'd just been single-handedly routed by a girl. Rose didn't care. She'd gotten rid of them, and that was all that mattered. They had no idea how close they'd been to danger. She turned her back on them and looked at Jade, standing there on the landing and watching the scene with inscrutable jewel-green eyes.

From a distance, she heard Ted's high voice. "Man, girls can be scary!"

"Not as scary as dragons," she muttered.

Chapter Four

A Dragon in the Living Room

Rose set down the pile of her mother's mythology books on her desk. Jade gave them an interested look and ran her fingers over the weathered spines. "There are lots of stories about dragons in here," Rose said. "Maybe I can figure out what to do with you."

But she didn't believe it. She had to admit she needed help. Jade was too strange too far outside anything Rose knew, and probably too dangerous for her to handle on her own. Who could she turn to?

Her friends? She trusted Lisa and had confided secrets before, but nothing like this. Clay would be willing to believe in a dragon. Yet neither of them would know what to do about Jade any more than Rose did herself.

Her father? Rose chewed her lip as she thought about it. Even thinking about that conversation with her rational, no-nonsense father made her palms sweat. She wished her mother were here and felt the sharp pain of her absence more than she had in years. Her mother, who had believed in angels and ghosts and all sorts of things her father scoffed at. She would've been able to cope with a real dragon...

An idea struck her.

"Come on," Rose said, grabbing Jade's hand. "We're going to see a friend."

* * *

Doris Jersey was not technically Rose's friend; she was a substitute teacher. Mrs. Jersey was warm, intelligent, quirky...and could make her voice crack like a bullwhip to bring an unruly class into line. More importantly, Mrs. Jersey had been a good friend of Rose's mother.

And she was rumored to be a witch.

This was common gossip around Boulder City. Old ladies at church would tut-tut when talking about Mrs. Jersey, grumbling loudly at the thought that someone so *peculiar* was allowed to teach children. Rose remembered her mother saying that Doris Jersey wasn't dangerous, she was just wise—and that most of the silly hens around town couldn't tell the difference. Most of the books about myths and magic in her mother's library had been gifts from Mrs. Jersey.

Rose hoped Mrs. Jersey would have something useful to tell her about dragons.

Mrs. Jersey's home was one of the bigger houses in Boulder City. With her husband passed away and her kids grown up, she lived there by herself, along with dozens of orphaned cats she'd rescued.

When Rose and Jade trudged up the long driveway to the big house, they found Mrs. Jersey in her colorful garden, being observed by an attentive Siamese cat. Rose lingered for a few moments at the fence, suddenly feeling uncertain about how she might confide that she'd made friends with a shape-shifting dragon without sounding like she'd lost her mind.

Mrs. Jersey seemed to sense she was being watched and looked up to where Rose and Jade stood at her gate. A kindly smile blossomed on her weather-lined face. "Hello there, Rose. How are you today?"

Rose returned the smile as best she could. "Hi, Mrs. Jersey. I'm good."

Mrs. Jersey set aside her gardening tools and peered at Rose through her round spectacles. "Are you sure? You look a little pale, dear."

Rose swallowed hard, still working up the nerve to mention she'd made friends with a real, live dragon. "It's nothing," she said, trying to sound casual. "Just some boys being dumb."

"Hmm," Mrs. Jersey hummed. "And who is your friend?"

"This is Jade. She's Dutch, so she doesn't speak much English." The lie came out before she had a chance to think about it.

"Oh?" The teacher smiled warmly at Jade. "*Aangenaam kennis te maken*, Jade."

Rose's jaw dropped.

Jade smiled blankly, then waved. "Weird," she chirped.

Mrs. Jersey raised an eyebrow.

The light-gray Siamese took the momentary pause in the conversation as an opportunity to make a thorough examination of Rose's left kneecap.

"You...you speak Dutch?" Rose asked.

"Some," the teacher said. "More than your friend here, I'm guessing."

Rose gaped, her mind floundering for something to say.

Mrs. Jersey subjected her to an uncomfortably piercing examination that seemed to drag on for a week. She brushed the dirt off her hands and gave Rose a reassuring smile. "Why don't you two come in and have some lemonade? I'm thinking there's something you want to talk to me about."

"S-sure."

"Very good." Mrs. Jersey turned and led them through her front door. The Siamese trotted after them, dislodging another pair of cats in the entryway.

About four of Rose's house would fit into Mrs. Jersey's home. A spacious hall opened into a living room so big that a school bus could be parked in it. What the room lacked in furniture, it made up for in bookshelves and artwork. Rose spotted a fearsome-looking mask made of red wood with an African spear underneath, lacquered statues of Egyptian gods with animal heads, a scroll with Japanese letters hanging on a mat of bamboo, a poster from the 1967 World's Fair featuring a large glass dome and a monorail, and all sorts of statues, paintings, and souvenirs from every corner of the world. Mrs. Jersey had clearly traveled a lot. Maybe it wasn't so strange that she knew how to speak some Dutch.

"Have a seat." Mrs. Jersey gestured at the plump cushions on her antique sofa.

Rose sat down and guided Jade onto the seat beside her. She kept a firm grip on the dragon-girl's hand to dissuade her from messing with any of Mrs. Jersey's decorations, some of which were probably very valuable.

"Two lemonades coming right up. And some graham crackers?"

"Yes, please." Rose felt a pang of worry that Jade would do something weird during what might be her first encounter with food as a human, but she was starting to feel hungry and thirsty. She had to let Jade eat sometime. Might as well start now.

A stout calico cat leaped up onto the sofa, purring at them. Jade watched it with open curiosity and giggled as it strode boldly up to sniff her nose. The cat let out a friendly meow, and Jade looked at Rose, as if asking her what to do next.

"Just pet it." Rose demonstrated, and the cat arched its back appreciatively.

Jade stroked the cat, and it rubbed its body against her. Satisfied, it flicked its tail and settled down beside them, purring softly.

Mrs. Jersey soon emerged from the kitchen with their snacks. Rose immediately picked up one of the glasses of lemonade and took a sip, making sure Jade got a good look at what she did.

Jade watched her and seemed to get the idea. She mimicked Rose's actions, and apart from dribbling juice down her shirt on the first try, she looked almost normal. Rose sighed with relief, then noticed the curious expression on Mrs. Jersey's face. She flushed, knowing that Jade's fundamental oddness had not gone unnoticed.

Mrs. Jersey moved to settle into a comfortable re-cliner occupied by an orange cat the size of a pumpkin. "Off, Jupiter," she said.

The cat swiveled an ear very slightly, just enough to indicate that it had heard her but chose not to listen.

"Move it, you lazy beast," she commanded and was again ignored. The authority Rose had seen Mrs. Jersey use in the classroom didn't seem to work on cats. With a long-suffering sigh, she reached down and shoveled the heavy cat onto the floor. It landed with a muffled thud, gave its tail a grumpy swish, and decided to pretend it had wanted to get off the chair all along. Mrs. Jersey settled into her seat and turned her gaze on Rose.

"Now, Rose. Tell me what's troubling you."

Rose began to speak before thinking. "Do you believe in..." she heard herself say, then snapped her mouth shut.

"Believe in what, Rose?"

"In...in magic?" Rose had been on the verge of saying *dragons*. She wasn't sure *magic* was much better.

Mrs. Jersey gave a chuckle. "Ah. Has someone been gossiping about me being a witch again?"

"Are you a real witch?"

"There's nothing so bad about witches," Mrs. Jersey said. "Members of the Wicca religion call themselves witches, and they're not at all scary."

"So are you one of those? A Wiccist?"

"Wiccan. And no, not really," she said, sipping her lemonade. "There aren't many in Boulder City."

"Why do people think you're a witch then?" Rose asked.

"Because I'm not afraid of knowledge other people find disturbing," she said. "And perhaps, to return to your initial question, because I do believe in magic."

Rose felt her heart skip a beat. "You do?"

"Let's be clear, Rose," Mrs. Jersey said. "I'm speaking to you as a friend, not a teacher. So I hope you know better than to approach Ms. Dawkins in your science class and repeat anything I have to say about the greater mysteries."

"Of course. I guess science is the opposite of magic."

Mrs. Jersey took another sip of lemonade. Somehow, a small green-eyed cat had appeared in her lap, though Rose hadn't seen it happen. "A common but unfortunate point of view. I believe that science and magic are fundamentally similar."

That wasn't something Rose had ever heard. "What do you mean?"

Mrs. Jersey raised a finger. "I'll give you an example. You have a smartphone, yes?"

Rose nodded.

"If I were able to go back in time and show that device to, say, Leonardo da Vinci, what would he think of it?"

Rose understood. "He'd think it was magic."

"Precisely."

"But we know better today."

Mrs. Jersey's face blossomed with a huge smile. "Do we? Could you explain to me how your little gadget works then?"

Rose opened her mouth, then closed it again. She might be able to say a few things about her phone—that it ran on a battery and had a touch screen—but she'd never even seen the inside of it. "I'm not sure. You're not saying it runs on magic, are you?"

"It's not supernatural," Mrs. Jersey said, "which is the spirit of your question, I think. A good engineer could tell us more, but I'll bet such a person wouldn't even mention the single most important thing that makes your phone possible."

"What's that?"

"Human genius," she answered, leaning forward. "The brilliance of all those designers and inventors whose combined effort went into the creation of something new and extraordinary. That's where the magic lies."

Rose turned this idea over in her head. It wasn't how she was used to thinking about magic. But she remembered how Jade had reacted when seeing a simple light switch in action and decided Mrs. Jersey might be on to something after all.

"So, what about other magic?" she asked. "Ghosts and spells and...stuff like that."

Mrs. Jersey studied her face. "Stuff like what?"

Rose gave an awkward shrug.

"I get the sense that there's something specific you want to ask me, and it's not a question about ghosts," Mrs. Jersey said.

Rose felt her throat go dry and took a swallow of lemonade. "Well, yeah. Something...something weird has happened."

Mrs. Jersey nodded and gave a curious look toward Jade. "Is this about your friend here, who isn't really Dutch?"

"Yeah," Rose said.

"And you don't know who to turn to. This is something you don't feel comfortable sharing with your father."

Rose gave her head a vigorous shake. "No," she said at once. She looked over at Jade, who was gnawing the end off a graham cracker. "I don't know what to do."

"My dear, I understand about secrets. Whatever you tell me, I will respect your privacy. All right?"

Rose met the teacher's gaze and felt her heart hammering in her chest. "This is very, very weird, Mrs. Jersey."

Mrs. Jersey did not laugh at her. "I suspect it is. There's definitely something odd going on with your companion, and I don't just mean her hairstyle. I can tell you this, Rose: I've traveled the world and seen strange things that most people in this town would not believe possible. I promise to keep an open mind."

Rose bit her lip, feeling her jaw muscles trembling. From a sense of desperation as much as trust, she made her decision.

She looked around the room, making a rough guess about the space available, then stood up. "I think I'd better show you. It'll be easier that way."

"If you like."

"C'mon, Jade," Rose said. She took the green-eyed girl by the hand and led her to the center of the living room floor, then backed her up to the entry that led to the hallway. There was plenty of room for a long tail to stretch that way, and the ceiling looked like it would be high enough. She just hoped Jade had enough sense to keep her head tucked down. She held up her hand to signal for Jade to stay and backed up until she stood beside Mrs. Jersey in her armchair.

"Okay." She pointed to Jade and threw her arms wide, beating them like wings.

Jade cocked her head from one side to the other.

"Rose," Mrs. Jersey said, "are you all right?"

Rose stared at Jade, then curled her fingers into claws and nodded expectantly. "Come on," she said. "Just like in the desert."

Realization dawned in Jade's green eyes. She gave a single nod, and Rose took a step back, holding her breath.

The air shimmered. The room seemed to waver, and suddenly the green-haired girl was no longer there. Rose and Mrs. Jersey stared up into the looming face of the dragon.

Mrs. Jersey let out a high-pitched yelp of shock and nearly toppled over in her recliner. At the same moment, a flurry of cats exploded in every direction. Rose hadn't realized how many cats Mrs. Jersey actually owned until then. Hundreds of claws scrabbled on floorboards and carpet as cats of every shape and size came shooting out from their hiding places, visible only as fuzzy blurs as they raced away.

Jade's hunched form filled the space, her great sinewy body folded in on itself to make her as compact as possible. Even so, she barely fit in the living room. Her serpentine tail twisted down the hall. She twitched her folded wings a little, toppling a chair and a small desk. Spiky ridges above her eyes flared out and scratched furrows in the ceiling as she tilted her head, showering herself with plaster dust.

"Okay, Jade," Rose said. She made a compressing motion with her hands, hoping to suggest shrinking. "Can you turn back?"

This time, Jade picked up on Rose's intentions immediately. The world swam once more, and then the girl stood before them again, the light green streak standing out in her long, wavy hair.

Rose stepped over to her friend and took her by the hand. Jade smiled at her and said her name. Rose turned back to face the astonished Mrs. Jersey, whose hair seemed to have leaped free from its tight bun to form a frizzy halo around her head.

"She's a dragon," Rose said.

Mrs. Jersey fanned herself with a hand. "Yes! My lord, so she is!"

"That's what I meant by magic."

"I see!" Mrs. Jersey fumbled her glasses back into place, her eyes wide. "Well, you do have a point. There's magic, and then there is *magic*!"

Chapter Five

What We Choose to See

After helping Mrs. Jersey clean up the spilled lemonade and soothe a few of the more irritated cats, Rose settled back into her place on the couch beside Jade. Mrs. Jersey had recovered some of her composure, even though her hair still stood up like she'd received an electric shock.

"So you said you've seen some amazing stuff," Rose said. "Have you met any other dragons?"

"No, no," Mrs. Jersey said. "Well, not that I know of! Jade can change shape, which means other dragons could too. Who knows? Maybe I have and didn't know it." She stared off into space for a moment. "That might actually explain some things..."

"But Jade doesn't act like a normal person," Rose said.

"No, that's true." The teacher examined the dragon-girl

with wide, interested eyes. "Did she tell you her name was Jade?"

"I made it up," Rose said. "I needed to call her something."

"Mmm, very fitting. There's power in naming, you know."

"Is there?" Rose said.

Mrs. Jersey gave her a keen look. "You sound skeptical."

"It's just...the 'names have power' thing sounds like something out of a fantasy story," Rose said.

Mrs. Jersey smiled, then cast a meaningful glance at Jade.

Rose had to laugh at herself. "Yeah, okay, so does a dragon. That's what keeps blowing my mind! Now I don't know what's real and what's imaginary. I used to know when something was just a story and when it was history or science. But now?" She bit her lip. "I don't know what to believe."

Mrs. Jersey leaned forward. "And how does that make you feel?"

Rose thought about it. "Confused, I guess. But it's exciting too. It's like the world has become"—she fidgeted, then spread her hands wide—"bigger."

Mrs. Jersey beamed. "Excellent, Rose."

"What do you mean?"

"We all face the unknown in our lives," Mrs. Jersey said. "We all find things that challenge our beliefs. It's easy to shy away and seek refuge in what feels safe when we fear what we don't understand."

"I'm kind of afraid," Rose admitted.

"Of course you are," Mrs. Jersey said. "Who wouldn't be? But you haven't given in to that. The world has become bigger for you. That's a wonderful thing."

"I don't get it," Rose said. "I'm not doing anything special."

"Oh, but you are. Do you know how many people choose not to see what is right in front of their eyes? I think not many people could have befriended Jade."

"I got lucky," Rose said.

"Maybe." Mrs. Jersey sipped her lemonade. "Why don't you tell me how you and Jade met."

Rose thought back over her day. "I think it started in art class," she said. "I drew a picture of a dragon today." Her anger over the ruined drawing simmered back up in her mind. "That idiot Trevor spilled paint all over it. On purpose."

Mrs. Jersey gave her a sympathetic nod. "Did the dragon look like Jade?"

Rose looked over at her strange new friend. "It kind of did," she whispered. "What does that mean? Did I...

predict the future or something?" The idea sounded so bizarre.

"I don't reject the possibility," Mrs. Jersey said. "You'd be surprised how much evidence there is for it. Maybe Jade was reaching out to you in some way. In any case, I think there's a reason Jade appeared to you. You're willing to see what someone else might overlook. Very much like your mother. She had an open mind to magic."

Rose fidgeted. She knew a little about her mother's beliefs...especially because they had been so different from her father's. She had a vague memory of asking about "horror-scopes" when she was six, triggering a rapid-fire exchange between her parents on the subject of astrology.

They hadn't precisely argued, not when she was there, but later in her bed, she had heard raised voices through her walls and got the impression from the few muffled words she could make out that they were talking about a lot more than horoscopes. The memory of her anxiety at overhearing her parents fighting still made her stomach tighten.

Her expression must have revealed some of what she was feeling, because Mrs. Jersey reached out and gave Rose a gentle squeeze on her hand. "Why don't you continue your story."

Rose nodded, glad for the chance to revisit the details of her extraordinary afternoon. When she got to the part about Jade's transmutation of the plastic dinosaur, she pulled the little figurine out of her pocket and showed it to the teacher.

"That's amazing," Mrs. Jersey muttered, turning the transformed triceratops over in her hand and running her finger delicately over its lifelike hide.

"What does it mean?" Rose asked.

"Not a clue," Mrs. Jersey replied, smiling as she handed it back.

Rose gathered her thoughts, then launched into the last part of the story, up to her showdown with Trevor and his cronies. "I was furious. They were ganging up on Clay, and Trevor was being so stupid..."

"And Jade did something then?" Mrs. Jersey said.

"Almost," Rose said. "I think she almost turned into... her real self. The air was shimmering, but nobody noticed except me." She remembered the sense of power and wrath she'd felt looking into Jade's eyes. "I stopped her before she turned."

"A good decision," Mrs. Jersey said. "And then you came to me for help."

"I thought about you when I was looking at my mother's old books on mythology," Rose said. "Do you think there's anything in those books that might help?"

"It couldn't hurt to look, but I think we'll need more than old legends." Mrs. Jersey stood up suddenly, a purposeful look in her eyes.

"What are you going to do?" Rose asked.

Mrs. Jersey stood and made her way to the other side of the large room, stopping before an expansive landscape of old leather volumes arranged on her bookshelves. "I think our first order of business is to communicate with Jade. We must find out why she's here, and why she chose to reveal herself to you."

"I wish she could speak English," Rose said. "I mean, she changed her whole body with magic. You'd think it'd be easy to pick up a new language."

Mrs. Jersey plucked a thick volume from a high shelf and thumped it down on the table. Jade approached and gave the book a curious examination. "Maybe. Maybe not. We don't know anything about dragons. Maybe it's easier for them to reshape their bodies than their minds."

Rose followed Mrs. Jersey around the room as the teacher selected volumes from her shelves—a bewildering variety of books with words like *divination, nonverbal communication,* and *archetype* in the titles. "What are you looking for?" Rose asked.

"Since we can't speak to Jade directly," Mrs. Jersey said, "I'm going to try gathering information in other ways. There are lots of different techniques I plan to try."

"What should I do?" Rose asked.

Mrs. Jersey turned to glance at the large grandfather clock standing in the corner. "When does your father expect you home, my dear?"

Rose looked at her own watch. "By dinner. That's pretty soon...but this is important!"

"So is your family, my dear."

Rose clenched her jaw and turned away in frustration. She wanted to argue but didn't want to risk offending Mrs. Jersey. The teacher studied her with sympathetic eyes as Rose struggled to come up with an argument that would allow her to stay and help with Jade.

Before she could make her case, Mrs. Jersey spoke. "This could take all night," she said. "And some of it will probably be very dull. Once I've gotten some of the groundwork done, I'll definitely need your help. But right now, you have something else you need to take care of." She looked Rose square in the eyes. "Do you intend to tell your father that you're friends with a dragon?"

Rose bit her lip and looked away. "I don't know. I

mean, I could ask her to change in front of him, like she did with you. That would prove she's real, right?"

"Yes," Mrs. Jersey said. "Is that how you want to break the news?"

"I don't know how he'll react," Rose said. "Can I have a little more time to think about it?"

"I think we can arrange that. Here's my idea. For the time being, I'll claim that Jade is a distant relative of mine." She flashed a conspiratorial wink. "A cousin from Holland, I think. She can stay with me as long as she needs to. That should give us time to figure out a way to communicate with Jade. Tonight, you go home, have some dinner, and get some sleep. Think about what you want to tell your father. Tomorrow, I'd like you to come by first thing."

"Before school?" Rose asked.

"You may need to miss school tomorrow," Mrs. Jersey said.

A surprised laugh burst from Rose, and she covered her mouth. "You're a teacher! You're telling me to ditch school?"

A knowing grin crinkled Mrs. Jersey's cheeks. "I believe I can arrange for an excused absence. You will make up any work you miss, of course."

"Of course," Rose agreed at once.

"It's settled, then," Mrs. Jersey said, clapping her hands together. "I'll see you bright and early tomorrow."

Rose gave a longing look at Jade before reluctantly setting off for home. Some part of her feared that if she let Jade out of her sight, the dragon-girl would disappear like a dream—and Rose's life would go back to being normal. The idea hurt like a stomachache.

Still, she knew Mrs. Jersey was right. She couldn't avoid going home tonight, not without worrying her father. The thought of him knotted up her stomach even tighter. She had her own life and kept some things from him, but she never outright lied to him. Not about anything important. She didn't know if she could pull it off now.

But what choice did she have, when he'd never believe her if she told the truth?

Chapter Six

Truth and Consequences

Rose's first plan was to act normal. She greeted her father at the back door as he came home from work. "Hi, Dad," she said with a cheerful smile, careful to sound as natural as possible.

His work boots creaked on the kitchen tile as he entered. He briefly examined her face, then glanced down to her shoes and clothes before looking straight into her eyes. "Something's up. What happened?"

Rose sighed. So much for acting normal.

That was her dad in a nutshell. When it came to things like her art, her favorite books and music, or her love of horses, he didn't understand her at all. But if she tried to hide something from him, suddenly his special dad powers kicked in and he could practically read her mind. He was like a cross between Sherlock Holmes and a brick wall.

Still striving to sound natural, she said, "I was visiting Mrs. Jersey. She's got family visiting. A girl named Jade. She's Dutch."

Her father rubbed his stubbly jaw and gave her a curious look. "Is 'Jade' a Dutch name?"

Rose shrugged. "Must be."

"Did you guys go hiking in the desert together?" he asked.

How did he do that? Rose wasn't ready to tell him the truth about Jade. With a flash of insight, she realized she had the perfect distraction in her backpack.

"No, I went alone. But look what I found!" she said, beckoning him to follow her to the dining room, where she had set her backpack on the table. "I picked it up a couple of miles or so outside town. You're not going to believe it."

"I won't, huh?" he asked, the hint of a smile on his craggy face. "Big geode?"

"Even better. Look at this." She withdrew the green teardrop-shaped stone and held it up to catch the light streaming through the window.

Her father's eyes widened, and the muscles of his face went slack. "Whoa."

Rose grinned. "I think it's a tektite..." she began, then trailed off. She'd forgotten how beautiful it was.

Flickers of sunlight danced across the ripples in its surface, while the gold flecks seemed to swim within the stone's translucent depths. Rose would've called it the most amazing thing she'd ever seen if she hadn't also met a dragon that day.

She reluctantly pulled her gaze away from the entrancing stone to see her father's reaction. He was staring like she had, just as mesmerized by the sight...yet she saw a strange expression emerge on his face. Was it...fear? But her father wasn't afraid of anything, certainly not stones. He loved them as much as she did.

His odd expression vanished as he wrested his eyes away from the stone. He gave her a sympathetic look. "It's pretty, hon. Probably not a tektite, though."

"Why not?"

"You don't find 'em around here," he said. "The nearest place you're gonna find a tektite is in Texas. Besides, it's too big. They're usually only a few inches long."

Rose frowned, certain he was wrong. "What is it, then?"

He took the stone and weighed it in his hand. "Melted glass, maybe? I don't know."

"But it *could* be a tektite," she said. "Maybe erosion unearthed a new deposit. It'd be a big discovery! Think of it!"

He held up his big, calloused hand in a calming

gesture. "Maybe. It's a long shot, though. Look, I'll take it to work and run it by Larry." Larry Stubbs was a geologist who conducted tours at the Hoover Dam. "He'll be able to tell us what it really is." Her dad must've seen the disappointment on Rose's face, because he squeezed her shoulder. "I just don't want you getting your hopes up."

She nodded. "Okay."

"That's my girl." He dropped the green stone into one of the pockets of his laptop bag. "How about some dinner? We've got leftover pot roast."

"Sounds good," she said, her mind whirling as she followed him to the kitchen.

Her dad was always like this—cautious, skeptical, never jumping to conclusions. That meant he was right most of the time. Was he right about the stone being nothing special? Maybe. But people did make amazing discoveries sometimes. Why was it so impossible for him to believe she could make one too?

Of course, she had made an amazing discovery today. She just wasn't sure what she could tell her rational, methodical father without sounding insane.

She puzzled over the question all through the meal and only followed the conversation with a fraction of attention.

"Isn't your class coming by the dam tomorrow?" her dad asked.

"Hmm?"

"Grant Ostrom said that Clay's social studies class is coming by on a field trip," he said.

"Oh." Rose remembered. "I'm in a different class," she explained. She didn't mention she intended to take the day off.

"Pity," her father said. "We're running the jet flow test tomorrow. You'd like that."

"Yeah," she said, not really following his words. The most incredible thing in her life had happened today, and she felt wrong hiding it from her father. But was it even worth telling him about Jade now? Maybe she should wait until she could introduce Jade in person and show him what she really was.

As if he sensed that Rose was thinking about Jade, her father said, "Didn't know Doris had family in Holland. What's the kid like?"

"She doesn't speak much English," Rose said. "But she's really friendly. I like her." She decided to test the waters by divulging a little of Jade's weirdness. "She has green hair."

Her dad made a huffing noise and sipped his root beer. "Don't you go getting any ideas."

Rose pursed her lips and tried not to glare at him. He always clamped down any time she wanted to do something he thought was inappropriate for a girl her age. She remembered the agony of getting permission to pierce her ears. He'd finally relented when she'd promised to only wear her mother's diamond earrings to church and on special occasions.

He could be so protective. Would that be how he'd react if she told him about Jade? Would he want to protect Rose from a dragon?

Maybe there was a way she could ask.

She set down her fork and focused her attention on her father. "Dad, what would you do if something weird happened to you?"

"Like what?"

"Like if you met...an alien, let's say. What would you do?"

He raised his eyebrows. "Somebody see another UFO?"

"No," she said. People saw UFOs all the time in southern Nevada. Her father insisted that most of them were experimental military jets out of Nellis Air Force Base, and that the rest were mirages, weather balloons, or regular aircraft seen from an unusual angle. He was probably right, but that wasn't the point. "Not a light in the sky or anything. What if you met an actual alien? In person?"

He shrugged his broad shoulders. "Probably call the government."

She gaped at him. "That's it?"

"Why not?"

"What if they put the alien in a lab and ran experiments and stuff?" In the movies, the government was always doing things like that.

He sighed. "All right. What would you do?"

"I'd..." She hesitated. "I'd try to make friends with it. Try to figure out why it's here. What it wants."

"Maybe your alien would be dangerous, Rose," her dad cautioned.

"But it might not be!" Rose said. "Don't you see how amazing it could be? How it could change the whole world?"

"Or threaten it," he said. "You don't know anything about this space critter. For all you know, its kind might be out to take over the earth. Or blow it up. If you chose to hide this alien from the authorities and it started hurting people, you'd be responsible. You're not ready for something that big." He shook his head. "Neither am I."

Rose stared at him.

He raised an eyebrow. "Believe me, first thing I'd do if some green, bug-eyed monster showed up on my doorstep would be to call the government and get it out of my hair," he said. "Hard enough to get by in this life without adding weird stuff."

She opened her mouth to say something, then closed it so hard her teeth clicked.

"What?" he asked.

"Nothing." She gathered her dishes and carried them over to the sink, glad to have a reason not to look at him.

"Come on, Rose," he said. "It's nothing to get upset about. I'm never going to meet a stranded alien, and neither are you. Right?"

She turned and forced a smile. "Yeah. I know."

By the time she returned to her bedroom, Rose had made up her mind. She couldn't tell her father about Jade, not in a million years. He'd think she was too dangerous. He'd call the government and they'd take her away—maybe to experiment on her or put her in a zoo. Rose couldn't risk that happening.

She spent the next few hours lying in bed reading about dragons, flipping through page after yellowed page of her mother's old books. After her eyes finally grew too tired, she drifted off to sleep with the book open on her knees, dreaming of long serpentine coils, vast wings silhouetted against the sky, and luminous eyes as green as emeralds.

Chapter Seven

Keyhole Canyon

Rose's father looked up from his morning paper when he heard a car pull up into the driveway. "Who's that?" he asked, leaning over the breakfast table to peer out the window. He was already dressed for work in his khaki slacks and faded-blue Bureau of Reclamation shirt.

Rose recognized Mrs. Jersey's little yellow compact, and her heart accelerated to a canter. She bolted down the last of her toast. "Mrs. Jersey said she'd give me a ride today," she said.

"Why?"

It was a fair question. Rose always walked to school, even on the rare rainy day. "I'm just helping her with Jade," she said, then darted for the door.

Rose greeted Mrs. Jersey with reflexive politeness, but she had eyes only for Jade. The dragon-girl was sitting in the passenger seat and waving excitedly. A giddy rush of relief and joy whooshed through Rose's whole body. Some part of her had been convinced that yesterday was some kind of dream.

"Hiya, Jade!" she said, then turned to Mrs. Jersey. "Did you have any luck communicating with her?"

"I think so," Mrs. Jersey said. She had bags under her eyes and her hair was more disheveled than Rose had ever seen, but she sounded excited. "If I'm right, we'll find more answers in Keyhole Canyon."

"Really?" Rose said. She knew the place—a slot canyon far out in the desert, accessible only by a long drive over dirt roads. "Why there?"

"I'll explain when we get there," the teacher said.

"Okay. Let me get my stuff."

Rose pelted through the kitchen and into her bedroom. She grabbed her backpack, chucking out her math book and checking over her standard "be prepared" supplies—water, first aid kit, binoculars, a tightly folded parka, and a few other necessities. She topped off her water bottle from the bathroom tap and darted for the door again.

"Easy there," her father said.

Rose skidded to a halt long enough to kiss him goodbye, impatient with every second she spent away from Jade. "See you, Dad."

He started to say something as she slipped out the door, but she only caught a few words. Was it about the tektite? It didn't matter. Her miraculous new friend was waiting, and Rose could think of nothing else.

* * *

The road out to Keyhole Canyon showed no mercy to small cars or their passengers. The unpaved service track that followed the power lines stretching from Hoover Dam to California was even rougher than Rose remembered, filled with countless new furrows carved by the recent rains. Mrs. Jersey's little car struggled along past the looming steel cable towers, kicking up dust and rattling the three occupants violently with every lurch and jolt along the twisting desert road.

After more than two excruciating hours, the three emerged sweat-soaked and aching into the silent desert air. Rose felt like she'd been on the losing end of a fistfight. Jade shot the car an extremely dirty look and made a huffing noise at it, which probably would have been really scary coming from a dragon.

"Sorry for the rough ride, ladies," Mrs. Jersey said, rubbing her hip as she levered herself out of the car. "Ooh. That stings."

"Are you okay?" Rose asked, moving to help her out.

Mrs. Jersey waved her off. "Old injury. Acts up

sometimes. The important thing is that we made it." She pointed toward a stark cliff face about a hundred yards away. "Keyhole Canyon."

Rose shielded her eyes against the midday glare, focusing on the shady region where the cliff split into the canyon. "What are we doing here?"

"This," Mrs. Jersey said, "is sacred ground."

Rose wasn't sure how to respond to that. She shot a look at Jade, who was rubbing her neck as she stared around.

"Come, help me with my things," Mrs. Jersey said. "I'll explain as we go."

The teacher hauled a large, round bag from her trunk, while Rose collected two canvas sacks full of books and what sounded like rattles. Jade watched this procedure with great interest, and eventually moved to help. She plunged her hands into the trunk and emerged with a looped mass of jumper cables.

"Um...I don't think we'll need those," Rose said.

"Here you go, Jade," Mrs. Jersey said, holding out a wicker basket containing a silver knife, some matches, and a number of squat beeswax candles.

They set out together toward the cliffs, the crunch of their footsteps distinct in the silence of this remote place. The clean desert air, so deliciously free of the fumes and residue of civilization, filled Rose with a sense of energy and purpose. But she kept her pace slow to help Mrs. Jersey, who moved at a slow limp with her sore hip. Jade trotted along on her own erratic course, veering between Joshua trees, tumbleweeds, and whatever else caught her attention.

"So what happened last night?" Rose asked.

"I used a number of methods and a bit of guesswork," Mrs. Jersey said, mopping sweat from her brow as the sun beat down. "Jade is eager to make herself understood, though it isn't easy. I believe she's looking for an object of great importance."

Rose's eyes widened. "What is it?"

"I don't know," Mrs. Jersey said. "But if I read the signs correctly, I believe it's important to all dragons, not just Jade. Ah, here we are. Blessed shade."

As they stepped into the shelter of the cliff wall, Rose looked up into the narrow fissure that marked the entrance to the slot canyon. Slabs of rock leaned against one another on either side of the cleft, forming a towering natural stairway on one face and several sheltered enclosures along the other. Rose could make out some faint scribbles on the sheer stone faces.

"Petroglyphs," Mrs. Jersey said, "For thousands of years, the native people of the land came to this place to carve these symbols into the stone. The shamans of the Paiute, the Shoshone, even others before them, all came to mark this as a sacred gathering place."

Rose moved in closer to examine the designs. The walls teemed with depictions of soaring ravens, leaping bighorn sheep, and plodding desert tortoises, as well as people dancing and hunting. Other glyphs were more like abstract symbols—rows of wavy lines, thatched patterns inside ovals, and squares with decorations that reminded her of a basketball court.

"What are we here for?" asked Rose.

"A place like this was used for ceremonies by generations of people," Mrs. Jersey explained. "We're going to hold our own ceremony to help Jade communicate with us."

Red rock gave way to gray as they made their way into the shelter of the canyon. The silence took on a new intensity beneath the towering walls, and Rose became acutely aware of the way her breath disturbed the near-perfect quiet. Every footstep whispered on the fine sand of the dry riverbed.

"I think this spot will suit our purposes," Mrs. Jersey said in a soft voice that sounded as loud as a shout within the eerie cocoon of silence.

"What are we going to do?" Rose asked.

Mrs. Jersey reached out to each of them. "Join hands now," she said. Rose took Mrs. Jersey's hand in her own and Jade's in the other to form a circle. "What we're here to do is strengthen the bond between you and Jade. If my divinations are correct, this will allow us to overcome the language barrier and meaningfully communicate with Jade."

Rose tried not to look as skeptical as she felt. "Isn't divination sort of like...fortune-telling?"

The teacher let out a small laugh. "Fortune-telling is mostly nonsense. Divination is more like well-trained intuition. Have you ever felt something was true in your heart or your gut, even if you didn't have evidence?"

"I guess." Rose said.

"Everyone has intuition," Mrs. Jersey said. "I've simply learned how to use mine more than most."

"How do you know this will work?"

"I don't," Mrs. Jersey said with a smile. "Ready to begin?"

"Okay."

Mrs. Jersey gave Rose's hand a comforting squeeze, then let go and got to work. She spread a small colorful blanket on the sand and set objects in place on its surface—a bowl of water, a black feather, a piece of petrified wood. "You might be wondering if all this really does anything."

Rose nodded, forcing a swallow down her dry throat. "All this" was the sort of stuff her father would scoff at as "mumbo jumbo."

"The energies that we call magic," Mrs. Jersey said as she lit one of the beeswax candles, "flow along channels. Like water. Each time a human mind performs a ritual, it creates a channel for that energy to flow. As people repeat the acts again and again, over the course of many years, those channels grow deeper and deeper. When we come to a sacred space like this and honor the ancient rituals, we invite power to flow through those channels. Do you understand?"

"Sort of," Rose said, toying with her hair. She looked around her, and the significance suddenly struck her. "Like the way a river will make a canyon!"

Mrs. Jersey beamed at her. "Exactly. What I'm really counting on is that we will activate Jade's magic to help us. No ritual of mine could suddenly allow two people who don't speak the same language to communicate. But with Jade..." She looked at the dragon-girl, who blinked back curiously. "With Jade, anything is possible."

Mrs. Jersey withdrew the silver knife from the wicker basket and traced a very simple circle in the sand around Rose and Jade. As they stood face to face, Rose felt a buzz of excitement in her belly. Was it just nerves, or was she somehow feeling all the currents and energies Mrs. Jersey was talking about? She turned to the teacher. "Now what?"

She unpacked a drum from the large, round bag. It wasn't like the prefabricated snare drums Rose had messed around with in music class. It was made of some kind of animal hide stretched over a circular wooden frame, decorated with faded symbols and patterns. "Now, I play the drum," Mrs. Jersey said. "The sound will help you relax and enter a kind of trance."

"Is this like hypnosis?" Rose asked. "Like when a Vegas magician puts a volunteer into a trance, then they walk on all fours and bark like a dog?"

Mrs. Jersey shook her head. "Nothing so dramatic. Technically you'll be in what's called the theta brainwave state. It's almost identical to what happens when you're really focused on something. Like your artwork. You know how it feels to lose yourself in the moment when you're painting, right?"

"Oh," Rose said, recalling her drawing of the dragon. "Yeah. Then what?"

"Focus on Jade. Feel your friendship for her. Look at her if you like, or close your eyes if that feels right. Let your thoughts flow."

"Like water," Rose whispered. She already felt like she was slipping into a trace.

"Yes," Mrs. Jersey said. "There's no hurry. Focus on Jade with your heart, and inspiration will arise."

"I'll try," Rose said.

Mrs. Jersey gripped her leather-wrapped drum beater and thumped on the hide surface of the drum. The thunderous voice of the instrument filled the silent canyon in a rush, each beat reverberating off the walls of stone. It wasn't music—just a steady, driving rhythm Rose could feel down to her bones.

Rose looked furtively at Mrs. Jersey, but the teacher had her eyes closed as she drummed. Rose turned to Jade, who stood with her head cocked in attention. Was the air wavering slightly around them, or was that just Rose's imagination?

She closed her eyes. At first she could think of nothing but the drum booming in her ears, but after a few moments, she hardly noticed the beat at all. She turned her attention inward, focusing on Jade. Focusing on dragons.

Images came to her. Pictures from the books she'd studied the night before drifted in front of her mind's eye, paintings and drawings of dragons made by artists from across the world. Legends of dragons appeared in every culture, every era. The Maya and the Aztecs portrayed them in vibrant colors, great serpents with feathery wings who ruled the skies as gods. In China and Japan, benevolent dragons were believed to grant wisdom to mankind and speak with the voice of the heavens.

Rose felt herself sway a little. The drumbeat pounded through the canyon and through her body, a counter-point to her own heartbeat.

More images from the books came to life in her imag-ination—dragons dancing and swirling through her head in a parade of long tails, sharp talons, and mighty wings. Some of the dragons in European myths looked liked Jade, but unlike Jade, they were deadly menaces. Rose remembered a painting by the Renaissance artist Raphael, showing Saint George on his horse fighting a strangely puny dragon not much bigger than a large dog. She thought of the dragon Beowulf had fought, a raging beast of wind and fire that had scattered the fiercest warriors and ravaged the countryside. Could Jade be that dangerous if roused? Or perhaps she might be like Fafnir, the treasure-hoarding dragon slain by the hero Sigurd, who then...

Rose's eyes snapped open.

"That's it!" she said. A pure, clear inspiration flashed

through her mind as suddenly as a bolt of lightning. "I've got it!"

Rose looked around and quickly spotted the object she was looking for.

Jade stared at her, and Rose could see excitement in her friend's green eyes.

Without leaving the circle, Rose reached out and plucked Mrs. Jersey's silver knife from the sand.

"Give me your hand," she said to Jade. Her voice emerged as a breathless rasp, but Jade understood quickly and put her hand into Rose's. Trembling slightly, Rose raised the knife and rested the ball of her right thumb against one edge. She guided Jade's hand until the dragon-girl had mirrored her position, their fingers intertwined and their thumbs pressed against each edge of the shimmering blade.

Rose spared a quick, anxious look at Mrs. Jersey. The teacher watched them with wide eyes, but she didn't miss a beat of her drum. She gave Rose a small nod.

Gritting her teeth, Rose yanked the knife up, slashing the skin of her thumb and Jade's in a single swift motion. With the knife withdrawn, their thumbs smacked together, blood from the twin cuts mingling.

Jade let out a little gasp of pain, and Rose heard a moan escape her own throat. She did what came naturally: she raised her thumb to her mouth and sucked on the wound. Jade did the same. Rose tasted the blood, hers and Jade's mixed together...

Rose's world spun out of control.

Chapter Eight

Jade Speaks

Some distant part of Rose felt her body collapse to the sand like an empty puppet, but she barely noticed. Her mind felt like it was caught in a tornado.

A cacophony of roars and howls and rumbles raged through her head, a great bewildering tumult of dragon voices. Yet as her mind was buffeted by one strange sound after another, she realized she could almost make sense of them. The dragon cries weren't words as she understood them—no rules of grammar or parts of speech like she might learn in a class. But they carried meaning. One thunderous roar caused an image of a volcano to bloom through her mind. A birdlike trill filled her with the joy of flight...On and on, dragon voices speaking, calling, whispering...

"Rose!"

She heard her name, as if spoken from an unimaginable distance.

"Rose, are you all right? Can you hear me?"

The riot of dragon voices in her head quieted at the sound of familiar English words.

"Rose! Oh dear..."

Rose forced her eyes open. The world swam before her in a blurry wash. "Wow," she said in a croaky voice.

"Oh, thank goodness!" Mrs. Jersey said. "What happened?"

Rose pulled herself up to a sitting position. Her limbs felt like overcooked pasta, but her vision was beginning to clear. "Sigurd," she said and smiled.

"Yes, Sigurd," Mrs. Jersey agreed, grasping the meaning at once. The teacher had probably understood the moment Rose picked up the knife. In the old Norse story, Sigurd was a hero who had slain the rampaging dragon Fafnir, then used the magic of the dragon's blood to gain the power to understand the speech of animals. When Rose had remembered that detail, her idea of what to do next had come in a brilliant flash.

"Jade?" Concern for her friend hit Rose like a jolt of electricity. She looked over to where the dragon-girl lay sprawled on the sand, her green eyes wide and dazed. Rose made her way on wobbly limbs to Jade's side and gripped her hand. "Are you okay?"

The dragon-girl sat up, blinking in confusion. She made a lurching attempt to get to her feet. Rose tried to help her, but both needed to lean on Mrs. Jersey to stand upright.

Rose looked into her friend's eyes. "Did it work? Can you understand me?"

"Rose?" Jade said. "I...understand..." With that, she plopped back onto the sand. The she let out a delirious giggle that echoed through Keyhole Canyon.

Mrs. Jersey gave Rose a concerned look. "Do you think she's all right?"

Rose nodded as she helped Jade recover her balance. "If she's feeling the same thing I am, it's kind of mind-blowing."

"Taking in a whole language at once?" Mrs. Jersey asked. "Yes, that would put some stress on the brain. Give it a moment." She gave Rose's hand a concerned look. "How is that cut?"

Rose looked down at the smear of red on the pad of her thumb. "I'll take care of it."

She retrieved her first aid kit from her backpack and began the familiar procedure of disinfecting and treating the cut. Working with horses had helped her get used to dealing with small injuries. "Your turn, Jade," she said when she was done.

Jade held up her hand, but when Rose cleaned the blood off the dragon-girl's thumb, she found no trace of the injury. "Hey! How'd you do that?"

"I heal fast," Jade said. She swayed a moment, then righted herself. She touched her mouth and smiled with wonder.

"You're talking!" Rose said, a huge grin spreading on her face. "It really worked! Mrs. Jersey, we did it!"

Mrs. Jersey squeezed Rose on the shoulder. "Well done, Rose. Let's take it slowly. Ask simple questions first."

Rose nodded. "Um...Jade, why are you here? How come you showed up so I could meet you?"

"Those aren't really simple questions," Mrs. Jersey said.

The dragon-girl pressed her fingertips to her forehead, squeezing her eyes shut like she had a headache. "Hard to remember," she said. "I-I lost something."

Rose stared wide-eyed at Mrs. Jersey. "You guessed she was looking for an 'object of importance'! Jade, what is it? What did you lose?"

Jade gazed around the canyon as if looking for something familiar. "It's a..." Her gaze settled on a chunk of rough stone about the size of a baseball. She picked it up and turned it over thoughtfully. "Like this."

"A rock?"

"Not this rock." She tossed the chunk of stone aside. "But a rock that's…" She pointed to her eyes.

"An eye rock?" Rose asked uncertainly.

Jade gave a single sharp shake of her head. She tugged a pinch of her hair, then pointed back to her eyes.

"Do you mean the color? It's green?"

"Yes! A green rock."

Suddenly the pieces fell into place. Rose gasped and leaned forward. "The tektite! You're looking for the tektite."

"The tektite? Yes!"

Mrs. Jersey looked confused. "Rose, what is she talking about?"

"It's a stone I found yesterday, right before I met Jade," Rose explained, then turned to Jade. "So it's really yours! What is it for?"

Jade rubbed at her temples. "Hard to remember. It's important." She made a frustrated noise. "I'll just ask the tektite. Where is it?"

Rose fleetingly wondered how her friend could ask a stone anything. "Dad took it to work. He said he was going to show it to a friend to figure out what it really is. I'll get it back tonight."

Jade's face went very still. "Your father has it."

"Yeah," Rose said. "Is that...a problem?"

Now Jade's expression turned grave. "It was made for me. If someone else tries to use it, it will protect itself."

A cold knot began to grow in Rose's stomach. "What does that mean? I handled it, and it was fine. It didn't shock me or anything..."

"Not like that," Jade said. She pursed her lips, as if struggling to find the right words. "It'll resist. Try to change his mind, I think."

"What do you mean by *use it*?" Rose asked, her heart pounding. "How do you use a rock? What's it do?"

Jade made a helpless gesture.

Rose clutched at Jade's shoulders. "Jade, tell me please! Is my dad safe?"

"I don't know!" The dragon-girl sounded almost as distressed as Rose. "Your dad isn't a dragon. I don't know how it will react to him!"

"Easy now, Rose," Mrs. Jersey said. "You said you found this object and it did no harm to you. If it was made by dragons, it's something magical. Your father doesn't even believe in magic. He wouldn't know the first thing about using something like this. I doubt it will perceive him as a threat."

Rose wanted to believe Mrs. Jersey's words with all her heart. "Jade...is she right? Dad just wanted to examine it to figure out if it's really a tektite. Will that set it off somehow?"

Jade squirmed. "Maybe?"

Rose couldn't be satisfied with *maybe*, not when her father might be in danger. "I've got to warn him!" She pulled out her phone and groaned in exasperation. "No signal!"

"Try again when we get closer to town," Mrs. Jersey said, then stooped to pick up her basket. "Come, Rose. Help me carry all this, and we'll head back to the car."

Every second they spent collecting the ceremonial objects wound Rose's nerves tighter and tighter. She grabbed her share of the load and ran for the canyon exit, willing Mrs. Jersey to move faster. At least Jade shared her sense of urgency. They raced ahead of the teacher, out of the canyon and over the stretch of desert toward the car.

"What do we do?" Jade asked as she kept pace with Rose, who moved in an awkward lope with her armload of supplies.

"Drive out to the dam," Rose said. "Get the tektite back from my dad before anything bad happens."

But even as she spoke the words, fear sounded its increasingly shrill alarm from within. She remembered the two creeping hours it had taken to traverse the choppy desert road—and even after that, it'd take at least another full hour to get to the dam. Three hours! She couldn't stand it. In desperation, she checked her phone again, but there wasn't enough signal to even send a text.

Even if she could get through to her dad, what would she tell him? He'd think she'd gone nuts if she blabbed about magic rocks. She groaned in frustration and stared north across the vast desert that stood between her and her father.

If only she could get to him faster. If only there was some way...

Her eyes shifted to Jade as if pulled by a magnet.

"It'll be too slow if we drive," Rose said.

Understanding dawned in Jade's green eyes, and she smiled. "I can go very fast." She looked back toward the canyon, where Mrs. Jersey was still moving with a limp from her sore hip. "Mrs. Jersey too?"

Doubled up and bareback on a horse, Rose might have risked it. But in the air? It would be dangerous even for one rider. Maybe too dangerous. She bit her lip and looked around uncertainly until her gaze landed on the jumper cables still lying in the sand where Jade had dropped them.

"I can make a safety harness with that," Rose said. "But not for two riders."

Jade grinned. "Just you and me." The air shimmered, the world swam out of focus, and a few moments later Rose was looking into the emerald eyes of the dragon.

"Hold still," Rose said.

As a dragon, Jade was far more massive than the horses Rose had ridden, but the jumper cables were long enough to stretch around her neck. Rose secured the thick black cable in place just above Jade's shoulders, tying her most reliable knots to secure it. Jade snaked her head around to watch her with one eye.

"Rose!" Mrs. Jersey called. "What are you doing?"

"Help me up," Rose said to Jade. She could feel her heart hammering in her chest, louder and faster than the drum in the canyon. Jade lowered her shoulder and made a stepping platform with her foreleg. A mane-like ridge ran along the line of Jade's backbone, rising above her back. Rose got a grip on it—the spines were more like feathers than hair, flexible to the touch and very tough—and hauled herself up to straddle Jade's neck. Living warmth rose through the dragon's armored hide, and Jade's powerful muscles shifted beneath Rose as she settled into position with her knees locked under Jade's wing joints.

"Rose!" Mrs. Jersey wheezed as she closed the distance. "Don't be rash!"

Rose couldn't let Mrs. Jersey dissuade her. Trying to steady her trembling hands, she hooked the dangling ends of the jumper cables to their anchor points—two on her belt, the longer two on the straps of her backpack. She looped them into place, tightened them, and fastened the clamps to reinforce their hold.

Rose steadied her grip. Her makeshift harness shifted, but it felt like it would bear her weight. She looked down at Mrs. Jersey from the height of the dragon's back. "My dad's in trouble," she said.

The teacher made soothing motions with her hands. "We don't know for certain he's in danger."

"I can't risk it," Rose said. "You know it'll take forever to drive there. This is the fastest way!"

Mrs. Jersey shook her head, then closed her eyes and took a deep breath. "Just...be careful!"

"I will!" Rose said. She tightened her grip on Jade's spines, her heart now thundering in her ears. Terror mingled with excitement at what she was about to do.

"Let's *fly!*" Rose sang out to Jade.

Jade let out a deafening roar. She spread her vast wings, kicked off with her hind legs, and suddenly they were hurtling together into the sky, Mrs. Jersey and her little car dwindling beneath them into tiny specks.

Chapter Nine

Hoover Dam

"This...is...*awesome!*" Rose shouted. Not even her worry for her father could overcome the thrill of flying for the first time. She threw her hands up and tossed her head back, laughing in delight as the wind whipped her hair behind her. Jade's mighty wings whooshed on either side of her with each stroke, translucent green skin glowing in the brilliant sunlight as they beat the desert air.

Rose couldn't have put words to the joy of it. She didn't try. It was better than riding a horse at a full gallop, better than *anything*. She whooped at the cloudless blue sky, savoring the speed, thrilling in the power, losing herself in the wonder of flight.

Jade spoke in a high, fluting warble.

A riot of impressions flooded into Rose's mind at once—curiosity, urgency, a need for guidance, all roaring in an overpowering jumble. The alien complexity of draconic language momentarily short-circuited her brain. Only her jumper-cable harness saved her from tumbling off the dragon's back.

Rose spoke, her voice more of a rasp and sounding miles away. "You...you want to know how to get there?"

The turbulent storm of her thoughts settled the moment she reached for a translation. This wasn't like speaking another language. She knew some Spanish, and it didn't knock her for a loop to hear it.

Jade let out a little grunt, the dragon equivalent of a simple *yes*, but it made Rose dizzy. Now she knew why Jade had almost fainted on her first attempt to speak English.

But Rose didn't have time for fainting spells. She leaned forward so Jade could hear her. "Follow the power lines. They'll lead us to the dam."

Far below them, their shadow whisked like a dark ghost over sage and sand. Rose peered to her left, eyeing the strip of highway. "Don't let anyone see us."

Jade banked to the right, veering farther away from the road. She let out a warbling question, trilling the sounds over the noise of the rushing wind.

Rose gripped the dragon's spines for balance against her disorientation and translated quickly in her head: *What do we do when we get there?*

"Good question!" Obviously they couldn't let Jade be spotted as a dragon. "We'll get close and land so you can change back. Then we go the rest of the way on foot."

The dragon made a little chattering noise. *Then what?*

"I'll get the tektite back!" Rose wasn't sure how she'd explain her sudden appearance at the Hoover Dam. She'd try to think of a reason. Even if her father got mad or punished her, all that mattered was to get the stone away from him. "We'll be fine if we hurry!" she said, willing it to be true.

In response, Jade pumped her wings, scooping great swaths of hot air with each beat to drive them onward. Rose leaned into the headwind, pressing herself against tough dragon scales, squinting her eyes against the wind as her hair swirled behind her.

* * *

"That's it." Rose pointed into the canyon below them. The brilliant white wedge of the dam came into view, stretching high above the rushing river. Jade veered toward it, but Rose pulled on her harness and leaned against the movement.

"Don't go directly at it!" she shouted. As much as she wanted to hurry, she didn't dare let Jade be seen in her true form. "Fly low on this side and keep out of sight. We'll come at it from behind, okay?"

Jade swooped down in the direction Rose had indicated, skimming low over the ruddy stone ridges to stay concealed. A few startled bighorn sheep bleated in panic as the dragon streaked overhead, then bounded away over the craggy bluff. Jade soared so close to the ground that she could have swept one up in her talons.

Rose adjusted their course, signaling by touch through Jade's supple neck spines. She angled them toward a spot where they could cross the winding ribbon of highway without much risk of being spotted and then scanned the bluffs and valleys for a place to land.

"There!" She pointed to a ledge on one of the towering cliff faces that looked over the dark-blue surface of Lake Mead. It would give them a good view of the dam without exposing them. "Set down there for a minute."

Dipping into the wind, Jade veered hard, sending them hurtling toward the cliff. She pulled up, beating her wings hard to arrest their momentum, and hovered for a moment before settling down onto the jutting shelf of rock.

"Get low," Rose said as Jade's claws touched down on solid earth. The dragon curled her wings up to her sides and hunkered down, the tip of her tail swishing in shallow arcs against the stone. Rose hoped nobody had seen them land.

This vantage point gave them a good look at the roads on either side of the dam. The Colorado River marked the border between Nevada and Arizona, and most cars crossed over a bridge that spanned the canyon a short way downstream. Only the employees and tourists drove down to the dam itself. Rose reached around and fished her binoculars out of her backpack. "I'm going to look for a place we can sneak in close to the road."

Jade grumbled something that carried both agreement and impatience.

"I'll be quick," Rose said. "Shuffle forward a little. I need a better look." She didn't want to waste time unfastening the cables of her makeshift harness to dismount.

Jade obliged her, belly-crawling her way toward the end of the rocky ledge.

Rose swept her binoculars along the road and over the dam. She hovered momentarily on the pack of her schoolmates on their field trip, noticing Clay standing slightly apart from the group and staring into the canyon with a daydreamy expression. As she shifted her focus in search of a good spot to land, her breath caught in her throat.

She saw her dad.

She recognized him in an instant—his long, muscular frame, his purposeful stride, his close-cropped hair under his work cap. She also saw the strange, glazed look on his face and the green stone in his hand.

He was walking toward the edge of the dam.

For a terrible moment, Rose's whole body went rigid, fearing what he might do at the edge of the seven-hundred-foot drop. But then she saw him toss the stone lightly in the air, its brilliant green surface catching the sunlight before it landed in his calloused hand again. Rose had seen him do it a hundred times in old footage of his minor league baseball days and during their games of catch in the park. In that instant, she understood what he was going to do.

"He's going to throw it," she said, letting out a shuddering sigh of relief. He was safe. The tektite hadn't hurt him. Whatever defenses it possessed must have hypnotized him to get rid of it. Her dad was being his thorough self, throwing the stone away where nobody else could get it.

Jade lurched into action so fast that Rose almost came off her back.

The world became a blur of rushing wind as the dragon launched herself into the air with a terrific leap. Rose scrambled for a grip and pulled herself flat against Jade's hide, saved only by the tough cables that held her in place.

"What are you doing?" she shouted.

Jade's reply pierced her like a hawk's cry. *I need that stone!*

Driving the translucent sails of her wings in a furious rhythm, Jade hurtled through the air. The strong tailwind from the lake propelled the dragon at a dizzying clip, but it was blowing in unpredictable, treacherous gusts. One powerful blast caught them as they picked up momentum, rocking Jade off her flight path and tossing Rose's hair in a blinding swirl around her face.

Rose clawed her hair away from her eyes and shrieked as she saw where they were headed. "The power lines! Look out!"

A spiderweb of high-tension wire crisscrossed the airspace around Hoover Dam, and the wind threatened to blow them directly into one of the steel strands. Jade had no way of knowing the extent of the danger—each of the cables carried enough raw current to reduce them both to a cinder.

The dragon dipped in the air at Rose's warning, diving to avoid one group of cables and nearly crashing into another. They darted so close that Rose could feel the buzz of electricity as it coursed through the metal, humming like a living thing.

Jade plunged away from the power lines and dived at one of the great intake towers, the stout cylinders of concrete that protruded from the surface of the lake and fed water into the Hoover Dam's power plant. She banked hard to avoid hitting the tower. A green wingtip dipped into the lake, kicking up a spray of white from the choppy blue water. Then Jade righted herself, leveling out just above the lake, and surged ahead with all her strength, gaining altitude to clear the lip of the dam. Rose held on tight as Jade's mighty wingbeats ate up the distance.

As they hurtled toward the dam, Rose could see her father rear back with the tektite in his hand. He planted his feet, put his whole body into the throw, and launched the glittering green stone out into the canyon.

No! Jade snarled with a furious rumble that shook her whole frame.

Rose held on tight as the dragon streaked over the dam, clearing the distance across the arc of the upper rim in the span of a heartbeat. They passed no more than ten feet over her father's head, and Jade tucked her wings into a power dive after the plummeting tektite.

Rose felt like she'd left her stomach hundreds of feet

behind. She didn't even have enough air in her lungs to scream.

The tektite glimmered in the sun as it plummeted. Rose could tell that Jade's angle of interception was slightly off. She wouldn't be able to reach the stone with her own claws or jaws. Only Rose would have a chance to catch the tektite in the split second its fall intersected their dive.

The sound of the air roaring in Rose's ears faded to insignificance even as it grew louder with each passing second. The dam, the canyon, the river hurtling up at them from below...none of it registered. Her concentration narrowed to a needle-sharp point until there was nothing in her universe except the tumbling green-and-gold tektite.

She let go of Jade's spines, trusting her legs and the harness to keep her in place. Reaching out with both hands, her fingers spread wide, she leaned into the furious wind, all of her focus on guiding the luminous stone into her grasp.

Her fingertips brushed the glossy stone, and then with a lunge, she had it in her grip.

Rose let out a whoop of exultation as she clutched the tektite to her chest, wrapping both arms around it. Her pinpoint focus vanished, and the rest of the world suddenly opened up again as if a curtain had been thrown back from her vision.

Her cry of triumph turned immediately into a strangled scream of terror.

The roaring in her head hadn't just been the wind. Rose stared into the canyon with wide eyes, horror clenching her heart. Impossibly huge columns of water erupted from the stone walls, each jet as vast as a freight train. Surging white torrents filled the air with their thunder, turning the path ahead into a cataclysm of liquid fury.

Immediately, she remembered her dad telling her that they would be testing the jet flow gates that day.

The series of cavernous tunnels that ran through the cliffs along the dam could be opened to drain excess rainfall from Lake Mead. The jet flow gates could dump thousands of gallons of water per second directly into the canyon beyond. Lake Mead hadn't come close to overflowing for years, but the Bureau of Reclamation still tested the gates periodically to ensure they would function when needed.

Rose had seen the bureau test the gates years before. She'd stood beside her father and peered out over the safety wall on the dam and had been awed by the sheer power of the tons of water blasting from the concrete portals.

Now she and Jade were about to fly directly into that nightmare.

Jade flattened out from her dive, skating over the choppy surface of the Colorado River as it emerged from the base of the dam. They were carrying too much speed to stop and were flying too low to pull up over the enormous torrents. If they were caught in one of the jet streams, they'd be torn to pieces.

Still clutching the tektite to her body, Rose threw all her weight to the right. She could see only one way through, a narrow patch of daylight between the crisscrossing streams.

Jade responded to Rose's signal, driving her way toward the deafening roar of water.

They shot under the first jet at a dizzying speed, the shock waves from the barrage of water so powerful that Rose could feel them rattle her bones. The turbulence knocked Jade off course, bouncing her toward the canyon wall and the path of a second jet. The dragon beat her wings furiously in an attempt to avoid the maelstrom of white water crashing against stone.

At the last second, Rose could see that they wouldn't make it.

She clutched the tektite to her with all her might as the wave hit her. Everything vanished in chaos as a wall of water slammed into her like a thousand wet fists. Rose felt her body thrown from her seat, battered in the merciless grip of the surge. Her attempt to scream only brought a lungful of freezing river. She tumbled, blind and choking, with no sense of where she was.

Suddenly, great claws wrapped around her body and held her fast.

A second later, Jade shot free from the frothing turmoil into open air. They had only hit the edge of the great jet's spray, but even that glancing impact had almost finished them. More fountains from the jet flows blasted from the walls ahead of them, but now Jade had enough altitude to clear them without danger. Rose coughed violently and wiped her eyes, watching the canyon roll by, cradled in Jade's strong claws.

She still had the tektite. That, at least, had gone right. She looked down at the green-and-gold stone clutched in her numb hands and hoped it was worth all the trouble.

Jade limped through the air toward a wide plateau Rose had spotted that protruded from the canyon walls about ten feet above the river. The cliffs would shield them from the sight of anyone on the dam or bridge, and Rose knew the river would be free of rafters and kayakers on a jet flow test day.

With awkward wingbeats, Jade came to a rest on the flat stone. She teetered on her legs long enough for Rose to detach the remaining jumper cable—which had probably saved her life—and dismount. The dragon thudded onto her belly to let out hacking coughs that sent convulsions along the length of her sinewy body.

Rose collapsed on the stone, trembling and wheezing for air as she watched Jade clear her lungs. The dragon soon began to emit bursts of steam with each breath. Jade heaved in one immense gulp of air, her flanks quaking with the effort, then belched out a brilliant burst of flame. The fiery stream raked the surface of the rushing river, sending up great hissing plumes of vapor. Jade smacked her chops a few times, let out another few smoking coughs, and looked much steadier.

So Jade could breathe fire. Rose smiled with delight in spite of her fatigue.

From back upriver, the din of water pounding against stone tapered off. The jet flow test was ending.

The reality of what they'd just done finally hit Rose, and a dull sense of despair seeped through her exhausted body. The tourists, her classmates, and her father had just seen her buzz the Hoover Dam on a dragon.

She and Jade were in for it now.

Chapter Ten

The Harbinger

For the whole flight back, Rose's anxiety had wound itself into knots as she wondered what would happen. There had been witnesses all over the dam. Her own father had seen her flying on a dragon. She hoped she'd gone by so fast that he hadn't recognized her...but what if someone got a picture? Could she be identified that way?

In any case, she had no doubt everybody had seen a dragon. Rose envisioned secret government agents poring over photos and videos taken by tourists, scrutinizing every detail on computer-enhanced enlargements to find clues about this mythical beast come to life. Jade was probably already all over the news.

At least Jade showed no signs of anxiety. The dragon retraced their path at a more leisurely pace, cruising above the cable towers as she soared over the winding service road from Keyhole Canyon. Rose saw a cloud of dust on the nearly deserted track and soon made out Mrs. Jersey's car laboring along.

Jade swooped in, and Rose braced herself for their landing, dreading the report she would have to give to Mrs. Jersey.

The yellow car skidded to a halt as they set down, and Mrs. Jersey burst out. "You're all right!" she cried out, relief on her face. Rose unhooked herself from her harness and dismounted, only to be swept up in a fierce embrace. "Oh, thank God," Mrs. Jersey said in a rusty voice.

The air shimmered, and Rose could feel the energy as Jade changed to her human form. Mrs. Jersey released Rose from her grip and reached over to clasp Jade's hand.

"What happened, Rose?" she asked. "You look devastated."

"Well..." Rose said in a small voice. "Dad tried to throw the tektite off the dam. I think it must've hypnotized him or something."

"Yet you seem to have gotten it back," the teacher said, looking at the green stone in Jade's hand. "That must be it. May I see?"

Jade held it out for inspection, and Rose heard Mrs. Jersey gasp at the sight of it. "It's incredible," she said in an awed whisper. "Beautiful...and powerful. It's almost as if the stone is alive." She shook her head, as though it took effort to look away. "Jade, what is it for?"

"It's called..." Jade began, and Rose felt a dizzying swirl of images whip before her mind's eye: a blinding light, a vast crater under a soot-black sky, dragons of all shapes and sizes bugling and roaring in confusion and dread. Rose reached desperately for the words to describe what she was seeing, what she was feeling...

"Harbinger," Rose said, and the images evaporated as quickly as they had come.

Jade swayed, looking momentarily as unsteady as Rose felt, then recovered. "Yes," she said. "Harbinger. That word will work."

Mrs. Jersey steadied Rose, who still felt a little disoriented. "Are you all right?" she asked.

Rose rubbed at her eyes. "Yeah." She gave Jade a curious look. "Did you just...read my mind or something?"

The dragon-girl shrugged.

"Harbinger," Mrs. Jersey said. "The word suggests a warning or an omen. Is that what the stone is, Jade?"

Jade turned the Harbinger over in her hands and frowned. "I don't know. It won't tell me more now. It's stubborn." She gave it a thump and shoved it into her pocket, then smiled at Rose. "Tell her about the dam!"

"My dad saw us!" The confession burst from Rose's lips in a moan. "Everybody at the dam saw Jade fly overhead. I bet it's all over the news and everything by now."

"Mmm..." Mrs. Jersey did not seem surprised by the information. "Let's see what we can learn from the radio."

Together, they all climbed into the little car, its engine still muttering in idle. Mrs. Jersey turned up the volume on the radio. Rose listened as the reporter rattled off local news items.

"—startling incident at the Hoover Dam today. An unidentified aircraft made an unscheduled flyover of the dam air space. Some witnesses described the aircraft as a UFO, a glider, or even a giant bird, but according to dam officials, the aircraft appears to have been an unmanned drone. The drone descended into the canyon and into the scheduled jet flow test, during which massive amounts of water are pumped from Lake Mead through bypass tunnels into the canyon beyond. Reports say the drone crashed directly into the surging waters. Officials at Nellis Air Force Base declined to comment..."

"A *drone*?" Rose couldn't believe her ears.

Mrs. Jersey turned the volume down. "I thought that might be you. I was..." She paused and put a hand to her chest and let out a trembling breath. "I was hoping the witnesses had exaggerated how close to the jet flow test you got."

"Very close," Jade piped up. She flashed a self-satisfied grin. She held her hands a few inches apart. "Almost didn't make it."

"Dear Lord." Mrs. Jersey closed her eyes and rubbed her temples. Then she reached out and gave Rose's hand another squeeze. "At least you're safe now."

"What's a drone?" Jade asked.

"Easier to show you, I think," Mrs. Jersey replied. "Let's get home." Her eyes darted to Jade's bulging pocket, where Jade had placed the tektite. "We have lots to talk about."

* * *

That afternoon, Rose munched on her sandwich and stared at the television screen in Mrs. Jersey's cozy den, watching as local broadcasters reported their version of the Hoover Dam incident. Only a couple witnesses had been quick enough to take pictures. One was a blurry image of the river with a triangular edge of wing in a corner. Another was of a distant green smudge against the canyon wall. The news then cut to stock footage of a jet flow test and several different models of military spy drones.

Rose felt a strange mixture of relief and confusion. "I don't get it. Jade doesn't look anything like a drone."

"I certainly don't," Jade said around a mouthful of sandwich. "I'm much bigger. And prettier."

"People see what they expect to see," Mrs. Jersey said, muting the television.

"Really?" Rose spread her hands wide. "But there was a giant dragon *right there* in front of everybody. Is everyone just afraid to say what they saw?"

"Something like that," Mrs. Jersey said. "Have you ever heard of unreliable witness testimony?"

Rose shook her head.

"Imagine you have a witness to something like a car accident," Mrs. Jersey said. "A blue car and a red car collide at an intersection. The police want to know who was at fault, so they ask the witness. The witness swears up and down the blue car moved first. She's willing to testify under oath. Then a video of the accident turns up, and—lo and behold—the red car moved first." She cocked her head at Rose. "Was the witness lying?"

"Uh...yes?" Rose guessed, then frowned. "But why would she?"

"It's not a lie," Mrs. Jersey said. "It's just that the accident happened too quickly for our witness's eyes to make sense of it. Under pressure, when asked to give her account, her mind filled in the blanks. Once it did, she firmly believed she had seen the accident unfold the way her imagination reconstructed it." Mrs. Jersey leaned back. "Everyone does the same thing to some extent. When we experience something we don't understand, our imagination leaps to the rescue to find an explanation."

"Even you?"

"Naturally. I strive to see clearly, but I'm only human," she said with a rueful smile. "I admire how clear your vision is, Rose. Not many people could have accepted Jade for what she is."

Rose thought back to her first encounter with Jade in the desert. "I almost convinced myself she was just a normal girl. That my mind was playing tricks on me."

"So you can understand how the witnesses on the dam did the same thing. In this modern age, we humans simply don't want to believe in dragons or in magic."

"You have magic," Jade said.

Rose and Mrs. Jersey looked at her in surprise.

Jade reached out and flicked the nearest light switch on and off. "Magic," she said. Then she ran her hand along the smooth wall. "Magic." She gestured at the silent television. "Magic." She spread her arms, a gesture that encompassed the whole house and the world outside. "Human magic is everywhere."

"But...that's just stuff we build," Rose said.

The dragon-girl shrugged. "So?"

Mrs. Jersey laughed. "Jade has the right of it. The things we do are just as marvelous to Jade as her feats are to us. To her, even a simple light switch is extraordinary."

"It's nothing compared to what she can do," Rose said.

"You might just as well call the abilities Jade has 'technology,'" the teacher said. "Human beings have become extraordinarily good at manipulating and working with certain forces of nature. We call it physics and biology and chemistry. Dragons have mastered different forces, ones that we think of as supernatural."

Rose took a bite of her sandwich as her mind gnawed on these unfamiliar thoughts. "Jade, can you tell us more about your magic?" she asked. "What is the Harbinger?"

Jade ran her finger over the glossy, patterned surface of the tektite, her eyes fixed on the green-and-gold stone. "It's still being stubborn," she said after a long silence.

"You said it was made for you," Rose said, keeping her voice gentle. The confusion she'd heard in Jade's voice worried her. "Do you remember who made it?"

"My mother," Jade said. Her usually cheerful voice was distant and dreamy. "Where is my mother? Where are all the others?"

"The other dragons?" Rose wasn't sure if Jade had been asking her or just thinking out loud. "I don't know, Jade."

Her friend gazed into the tektite for a few seconds longer, and Rose thought for a moment she might say more. Then Jade set the Harbinger down on the little coffee table next to her empty lunch plate, picked up the little calico cat that had befriended her, and snuggled into the plush embrace of Mrs. Jersey's couch. "Tired," she said with a huge yawn, and curled up with the cat cradled in her arms.

"Wow," Rose said as Jade's snores mingled with the cat's purrs.

Mrs. Jersey sighed. "Dragons are said to be legendary sleepers."

This was true enough—Rose's borrowed books had plenty of references to dragons sleeping away the years in their lairs. Instant slumber must've been another of Jade's superpowers. "Do you think she's okay?"

"It's natural for her to be tired after her adventure today," Mrs. Jersey said.

"I mean her memory," Rose said. "I thought she'd

be able to answer all our questions once we figured out how to talk with her, but it's not working that way."

"Learning a language that fast might have shocked her mind," Mrs. Jersey said. "Also consider the effects of changing into a new body."

"Oh." Rose had read enough fantasy books about the dangers of shape changing. She remembered that in *A Wizard of Earthsea*, the main character turned into a falcon for too long and forgot he was a man. Maybe turning into a human had messed with Jade's brain too. "What can we do to help?"

"I don't know," Mrs. Jersey said. "This is new territory for me too. All we can do is be patient and hope she recovers her memories."

"Maybe I'll find something in my books," Rose said, gathering her things to go home. "I'll be back tomorrow." She paused at the doorway. "Do you think everybody at the dam will really say it was just a drone?"

"If they don't," Mrs. Jersey asked, "who would believe the truth?"

* * *

After all the danger and magic of the last twenty-four hours, Rose thought there was something bewildering about walking home along the same sidewalks she had seen her whole life, along the streets of her utterly normal, familiar hometown. Boulder City hadn't changed since yesterday. Yet Rose now felt that she saw the world in a whole new way.

She brushed her fingertips over the pitted cinder blocks of a garden wall, the rough concrete tickling the soft pads of her fingers. She leaned back and breathed, the hot breeze carrying the desert scents of sage and creosote to her nostrils.

There were mysteries everywhere. She felt this deep in her bones now. There was meaning hidden in the wispy edge of a cloud passing overhead. The chittering of the sparrows as they flitted through the gaps in a chain-link fence held some deeper message, some barely glimpsed code. Everything had a secret to tell her—every gust of wind, every splash of water, every shadow cast on the concrete—if only she knew how to look and listen with an unclouded mind.

She walked slowly, drinking in the familiar territory with a new sense of wonder. She felt as if someone had turned the dials up on all her senses, sharpening her eyes and ears to superhuman acuity.

Perhaps that was why she spotted the figure hunched in the alley before he saw her.

Rose froze. She could see the barest edge of a shadow against the asphalt. Somebody was crouched behind the trash cans in the alley behind her house.

Her immediate suspicion was that Trevor Wallace was hiding in preparation for another of his stupid jokes. "Who's there?" she called out in her best commanding voice.

The shadow jerked the moment she spoke. She heard the scrape of tennis shoes on gravel, and then Clay Ostrom poked his head from behind one of the bins.

The tension went out of her at once. "Clay?" she asked. "What are you doing back there?"

Clay stepped out, cast a furtive glance over his shoulder, and beckoned her to come a little closer. "I ran away from home," he said.

"You *what*?"

"Not for good or anything," he added hastily, his voice barely above a whisper. His eyes were red and puffy like he'd been crying. "My dad grounded me for talking back to him."

"About what?"

"About what I saw at the dam today."

A startled jolt shot down the length of her spine. She took a hard swallow. "Oh yeah, I heard about that. Was it some kind of drone or something?"

Clay twitched like she'd jabbed him with a needle. "I saw what I saw today at the dam, and it wasn't a drone.

It was a *dragon*, Rose. Like the one you drew."

She didn't say anything. She knew she should probably tell him that was ridiculous, but she couldn't bring herself to.

"There was a person too," he said. "Someone riding the dragon. It looked like a girl with long, red hair." He glanced at her hair, then looked back into her eyes. "I saw it, Rose. Nobody believes me. Tell me you know what I'm talking about. Please."

She tried to think of something to say.

"*Please*," he whispered.

Rose couldn't bear to lie to him anymore. "Look, you have to promise not to tell anybody."

Clay let out a noise somewhere between a sob and a whoop of joy. "I knew it." He pumped his trembling fits in an awkward, triumphant gesture. "I *knew* it! It was real!"

"Yeah, she's real," Rose said, making shushing motions.

"Wait, wait...*she*?" Clay's eyes widened behind his glasses.

"Her name's Jade. You met her yesterday. She can turn into a girl when she wants to."

Clay clapped his hand over his mouth. "Oh God. Oh God. Oh God. I met her! I met the dragon!"

"Remember, you can't tell anyone," Rose said and frowned at the sudden look of guilt on Clay's face. "Did you tell someone?"

"Everyone at the dam saw it," Clay said defensively. "I mean her. Everybody just stared after you guys flew by, and then my dad was there, and he said it must've been a drone. And then everyone was like, 'Oh yeah, that makes sense!' It was crazy! How could they not admit they'd just seen the most amazing thing ever? I told them it was a dragon, and they said I was making things up!"

Rose sighed and stared at the sky. She knew all about Clay's temper, especially in the face of an accusation like that. "Then what?"

"I got sent to the counselor's office," Clay said. "Trevor and his idiot friends are posting online everywhere about it, calling me 'dragon boy.'"

That was so typical—those bullies never missed a chance to rub it in. Rose put a hand on her friend's shoulder. "Well, guess what, Clay. You are a dragon boy now. Jade's real. And she's gonna need our help."

Clay lip quivered as if he didn't dare believe what he was hearing. "All my life," he said, "I'd read books about magic and heroes, and then I'd look around at the boring old world we live in..." He took a deep, shuddering breath. "The only thing I ever prayed for was that if there was anything out there that was different or supernatural, anything magical...that it would happen to me. Good or bad. I wanted it to happen to me." He smiled at her. "Did you ever feel that way?"

"Yeah," Rose said. Who could read all those books about fantastical places and magical creatures and not wish for them to be real? "I guess your wish got answered."

Clay let out a joyous laugh. "Yes. Yes! A real dragon. And you said she needs our help?"

"Come on," Rose said, gesturing for him to walk beside her. "I'll tell you all about it."

Interlude

In a vast room, a figure sat alone in front of a computer monitor. Through towering windows that lined the walls, the last purple radiance of the setting sun faded into black. A pulsing tide of multicolored light from the Las Vegas strip flooded through the glass, mixing with the glow from the monitor to illuminate the man's handsome features.

He stared at the screen, seeing the message that nobody else could see.

Plenty of people had visited the web page, obvious from the growing number of comments that stretched out in a tail beneath the original article. Lots of people had opinions to offer, outrage to express, or wisecracks to make about the story of a rogue military drone destroyed at the Hoover Dam. None of them had anything of value to say, save one: a single post from

"TWallace_Rulez," buried among those from all the rest who had come by to throw in their worthless two cents.

"Clay Ostrom says it was a dragon," the post declared. "Call the guys in white coats!"

The man in the office tapped his finger against his chin and read the words again.

Change was in the air. He felt it, as he had always been able to feel such things. Now he understood much of what was going on—and he needed to know more. This could be the moment he had been awaiting for so very, very long.

The name in the post struck a chord of recognition. "Clay Ostrom," he murmured. He knew an Ostrom. Perhaps there was a connection he could follow.

Things would fall into place, as they so often did for him. In this town of gamblers and dreamers, luck was his domain.

Rex Triumph smiled and picked up his phone.

Chapter Eleven

Water and Earth, Air and Fire

The Harbinger sat on the round patio table, mystifying and beautiful as always in the fading evening light. Rose sat with Jade and Clay on either side of her, staring into the tektite's green-and-gold depths as if she could pry information out of it through sheer force of will. Jade wore the same distant, somewhat confused look she always did when contemplating the object that held the answers to her purpose.

Only Clay still wore a smile. "Hey," he said, pointing at the circular table top. "We're like the Knights of the Round Table. And that's the Holy Grail!"

"What about Mrs. Jersey?" asked Rose.

Clay grinned at her as if he'd been hoping she'd ask. "She's our Merlin!"

Jade cocked her head with kitten-like curiosity. "Who are these knights?"

Rose tuned Clay out as he gleefully launched into an explanation of the legend of King Arthur. It was a nice idea, but unfortunately they didn't know what their own grail was supposed to do. Worse, Mrs. Jersey wasn't having any luck as their Merlin. The teacher had been working day and night with her divinations, mediations, and vision quests, but so far she hadn't come up with anything helpful. Rose glanced at the big house. A somewhat frazzled Mrs. Jersey had sent them out into the yard earlier for some peace and quiet while she tried another of her rituals.

Jade absorbed Clay's story with delight, peppering him with questions about armor and jousts and the code of chivalry until even he ran out of steam. "It's a great story," he finally said, "but can we get back on track? We really need to figure out your Harbinger, right?"

Jade sighed at the sky—a mirror of one of Rose's own gestures of frustration. "I know. It's hard! I feel like there's a memory just out of reach." She gave the stone a black look. "*You* could be more helpful," she told it.

Rose knew the feeling Jade was talking about, like a word was on the tip of her tongue. "Maybe we could do something to jog your memory," Rose suggested.

"Yeah!" Clay said, leaning forward. "Like, we could

guess what the Harbinger is for. If we guessed right, do you think you'd remember?"

A playful smile crossed the dragon-girl's face. "Is this a game?"

Clay shrugged. "Uh...kind of."

Jade leaned forward, her green eyes glittering. "Right! You get three guesses. If you guess right, you win. If you don't guess, I win." She tilted her head back and forth, considering. "Let's see...if I win, I get your phone. What do you want if you win?"

Clay's shocked expression perfectly mirrored the sense of bewilderment Rose felt. "Why do you want his phone?" she asked.

"He looks at it a lot, so it must be interesting," Jade said. "But I'd really rather lose so I would know what the Harbinger wants." She turned back to Clay. "So, what do you want if you win?"

Clay scratched his head. "How about I get to fly with you?"

"Done!" Jade said. "Okay, now guess."

Clay gave Rose a helpless look, but she only shrugged. Jade had the bit in her teeth now. "Okay," he said, twisting his hands in front of him. "Is it a weapon?"

Jade laughed. "Why would any dragon make a weapon that someone else could take away?"

Clay ran his fingers through his curly hair. "Uh...is it a key?"

"A key to what?"

When Clay looked stumped, Rose spoke up. "Treasure?"

Jade shook her head, almost regretfully. "If a dragon wants to hide something valuable, they don't make doors and keys."

"Right," Clay said. "Last guess." He looked at the Harbinger as if fishing for inspiration, then finally spoke up. "Is it...a dragon egg?"

Jade leaned back, startled. "Our eggs don't look like rocks! Do yours?"

Clay's face went tomato-red, and he made a choking noise.

"We don't hatch from eggs," Rose said with a laugh. "Our mothers give birth to us."

Jade cocked her head as she processed this information. Rose got a hint of the eerie sensation she'd experienced when she'd first named the Harbinger. Images quickly shuffled through her mind of mothers, infants, and school lessons about human biology—like Jade was pulling the knowledge directly from Rose's own memory. The dragon-girl's eyes grew wider and wider. "Oh," the dragon-girl said. "*Oh!*"

Rose felt her own cheeks heating up. "So I guess it's not going to hatch any time soon," she said.

"I don't think so," Jade said with a sly grin. "We could build a nest just in case."

"We'll take turns sitting on it," Rose said and broke into a fit of giggles.

Jade joined her, adding her exuberant chime of a laugh to Rose's own.

Clay laughed along in a kind of nervous, forced way. "So...I lose, huh?" he asked.

Jade fixed him with an unblinking look and held out her hand, palm up.

Clay swallowed hard, then slowly drew his phone out of his pocket and handed it over.

The dragon-girl poked at the screen while Clay looked on with a sick look on his face, probably wondering what he was going to say to his parents.

As funny as his basset hound expression was, Rose felt sorry for him and wondered if she could get Jade to return her prize. "I didn't know you liked guessing games," she said.

Jade looked up. "Dragons like lots of games. We play them for fun or to settle arguments or for territory."

"You don't just fight?" Clay asked.

"Of course not!" Jade said. "That'd be too dangerous.

And uncivilized."

Clay opened his mouth to say something when the phone in Jade's hand chimed. The dragon-girl turned it this way and that in interest. Clay cleared his throat. "Um, that means I've got a text message."

"Oh," Jade said and handed the phone back to him.

"Can I keep it?" he asked anxiously.

To Rose's relief, Jade answered with a gracious nod. The troubled lines in Clay's brow smoothed away as he exhaled heavily. Then a puzzled look crept across his face as he read his text. "It's from Uncle Scott," he said. "He wants to take me somewhere."

"Where?" Rose asked.

"I dunno. He says it's a surprise. Weird." Clay pursed his lips and gave the tektite an exasperated look. "I've gotta run. Maybe Rose can come up with some better guesses. Something's bound to trigger your memory."

Jade simply shrugged. Rose waved good-bye to Clay and told him to leave through the garden gate so he wouldn't disturb Mrs. Jersey. That left just Rose, Jade, and the silent green stone.

No matter how hard she tried, Rose couldn't come up with a single guess about what the tektite could be for. "I wish Clay had won your game," she said.

Jade planted an elbow on the table and leaned her

head against her fist. "Me too. He would've liked to fly."

"Maybe some other time we'll..." Rose trailed off as an idea suddenly bubbled up to the surface of her thoughts. "Hey! Let's go now!"

Jade perked up and gave her a quizzical look.

Rose couldn't believe she hadn't thought of this before. "You say the Harbinger should tell you what it's for, but it's being stubborn. What if the problem is that you're human? Maybe you can talk to it better as a dragon!"

Excitement lit Jade's eyes. "That might work!" Jade got to her feet and picked up the stone. "I want to take it flying. It helps me think."

A thrill of anticipation traveled like electricity through Rose's body. For a brief moment her desire to fly warred with her caution about being spotted. "It should be fine if we're careful," she said.

Rose led Jade to the large open space in the backyard, safely away from the gazebo and Mrs. Jersey's vegetable garden. "Okay," Rose said, surveying the sky. To the west, the dusty-pink remnants of sunset glowed over the mountains. They'd be taking off in near-darkness from the top of a hill, which she thought reduced their chances of being spotted. "Head due east toward the canyon. That'll take us out of town and over open desert where nobody will spot us. Sound good?"

Jade turned to her with eager eyes and nodded. "Yes!"

Rose felt the familiar shifting sensation of the world swimming out of focus as Jade transformed. The dragon stood before her, eyes shining with a faint inner luminosity, as if reflecting the light of emerald-green fire. Rose stroked the length of the dragon's jawline as Jade lowered her head to give her an affectionate nudge.

With a step up from Jade's foreclaw, Rose vaulted onto the dragon's back. "No crazy stunts or anything this time," she said, securing her grip on the pliant spines on Jade's withers. "We're bareback."

Are you ready? Jade asked in her fluting dragon voice.

Rose could feel her heart racing with anticipation, a rhythm that felt like a counterpoint to the silent, beckoning call of the dusk sky. "Take us up!"

With that, Jade launched herself into the air, leaving Mrs. Jersey's home dwindling beneath them as they ascended at an incredible rate. Rose leaned forward onto Jade's neck until she was almost flat, feeling the dragon's great muscles flexing as Jade pumped her enormous wings.

Rose looked back over her shoulder as Jade leveled off, relishing the sight of her sleepy little hometown shrinking in the distance. Right now her classmates were watching TV or playing video games while she soared through the skies on the back of a dragon. What would they say if they knew? Some foolhardy part of her wanted to tell Jade to turn back and swoop low over the houses and roar with all her might, just so they could watch Rose's friends and neighbors stagger into the street and gape in awe.

Suddenly the world lit up under the glare of a powerful spotlight.

Rose wrenched herself around and immediately shielded her eyes against the light. Now she could hear a distinct noise over the rushing wind of their flight: the unmistakable *whup-whup-whup* of a helicopter rotor. Her heart seemed to freeze. They weren't alone in the air.

"Dive!" Rose shouted. "Get out of the light!"

Jade responded quickly, folding her wings and dropping out of the beam.

Rose let out a shriek as the sudden maneuver nearly pulled her off Jade's back. Rose's legs actually left contact with Jade's hide as her body flailed like a flag, anchored only by her desperate grip on the spines on the dragon's neck. She'd had horses come out from under her before, but a four-foot drop to sand from horseback was nothing like losing her seat at their altitude. "Stop!"

she howled, her fists clenched tight enough to crush walnuts. "I'll fall!"

With an apologetic grumble, Jade pulled out of her dive and smoothed her flight path. Rose hauled herself back into her seat, her legs clamped hard against the dragon's sides. She took in huge gulps of air as adrenaline sizzled in her blood. She had the presence of mind to look back at the helicopter, now hovering at a higher altitude a couple of hundred yards away.

What was it? Jade asked.

"A helicopter tour coming back from the Grand Canyon," Rose replied. She pressed her forehead against the warmth of Jade's hide, feeling foolish for not having thought of the possibility of crossing paths with a tourist flight. "Can we set down for a little bit? I need to catch my breath."

Jade wheeled into a more controlled descent. *Are you okay?*

"Yeah." They'd been spotted again, but only for a few seconds.

Rose watched as the helicopter hovered for a few moments, then tilted and resumed its path back to Boulder City. With any luck, only the pilot had seen them for a brief moment.

Rose was grateful for Jade's feather-soft landing

on the desert floor. She slid off the dragon's back and landed on wobbly feet, her hands aching from clutching Jade's spines so tightly. "That was too close," she said.

Jade craned her neck to peer back at her. *Will there be trouble?*

"I hope not," Rose said. "Whoever saw us will probably react like they did at the dam and think we were something like a small plane or a powered glider." She leaned her back against her friend's flank and looked up into the deepening blue of the evening sky. "I don't know how other dragons manage to stay hidden all their lives."

We wouldn't hide, Jade said.

"What do you mean?"

Rose's body rocked gently as Jade drew in a long breath. *There are many kinds of dragons,* she said. *There are dragons of water, earth, and air.*

As the musical cadence of Jade's speech washed over and through Rose, images coalesced in her imagination. A misty parade of dragons flowed through her mind—serpent-like dragons undulating smoothly through the endless sea; armored, flightless dragons shaking the earth with the thunder of their footfalls; elegant dragons with six wings and glorious feathers racing among the clouds.

There are dragons of fire, like me, Jade said, and for an instant Rose saw flashes of others like her friend. Most were larger than Jade, some so huge their translucent wings rivaled the span of jumbo jets, and all exuded an invisible sense of raw power like the heat off a bonfire.

We are all different, Jade sang. *We are proud and solitary. But we are not shy.* She locked one radiant green eye on Rose. *Dragons take territory and rule it. If we were among you, we would not stay hidden.*

As she pulled back from the dizziness of translating so much dragon speech, Rose realized she'd made an assumption about dragons since she'd met Jade. She'd thought dragons were rare, reclusive beings who used their powers to disguise their true nature from human beings, just as Jade did. But the world she'd glimpsed had been *filled* with dragons. There was no way so many could go unnoticed.

"Where do you come from?" Rose asked, and her voice came out in a creaky rasp. "Are you even from our world?"

The rumble from deep in Jade's chest carried as much confusion as Rose felt. *I don't know. All I know is this is not the world I remember.*

"But...you're not trying to take territory and rule it," Rose said with a nervous hitch.

No, Jade agreed. *I'm young. A fledgling. When we are young, we flock with our nest mates and others our age. Only when we become adults do we set out on our own to seek territory.*

"Oh," Rose said, biting her lip. "So...does that mean you'll leave me when you grow older?"

Never.

The single word felt like coming into a warm home from the freezing cold. Rose pressed herself hard against Jade's side, wishing she had arms long enough to hug a dragon. Jade curled herself more tightly around Rose, sheltering her with wing and tail.

Eventually, Rose remembered the reason for their flight. "The Harbinger," she said. "Is it...um...talking to you now?"

Jade held the tektite up in her foreclaw so they could both see it. *No,* she said. *It's as stubborn as ever.*

"It was worth a try."

Somehow, Rose didn't feel the same sense of disappointment she'd experienced after their previous failures to decode the mystery of the stone. Jade's words echoed again in her mind: *Dragons take territory and rule it. If we were among you, we would not hide.* A shudder passed through her, a chill that even Jade's warmth could not protect her from. Right now, asking what the Harbinger was really for didn't seem so safe.

As Rose mounted up again and prepared to head for home, she wondered if it might not have been better to let her father throw the tektite away after all.

Chapter Twelve

Lost World

Rex Triumph surveyed his domain from the vantage point of his hidden platform overlooking the Lost World promenade, waiting for his guest to arrive. The panorama of his casino spread before him filled him with satisfaction, as it always did. His will and ingenuity had created a place that outclassed other resorts like the Excalibur with its knights and armor, the Egyptian-themed Luxor, and the faux-classic architecture of Caesars Palace. Las Vegas was a city of wonders, and nothing compared to the sprawling artificial jungles and majestic animatronic dinosaurs of Triumph's achievement.

Not bad for someone who was a mere shadow of himself.

Triumph passed his gaze across the grand lobby of Lost World, scanning the teeming humanity. Walking beneath the entryway with the soaring pterodactyl suspended above the doors came the two figures he sought. One was familiar to him—Scott Ostrom, an enthusiastic and valued employee, especially invested in the construction of Triumph's second great casino.

But just now, Scott was only the deliveryman. Rex Triumph's real interest was in the skinny, curly-haired thirteen-year-old boy who walked beside him.

Clay Ostrom, the boy who had seen a dragon.

Triumph watched as the pair passed through the vast Mesozoic forest that enfolded all the shops, restaurants, and casinos on the first three levels of the hotel. He'd seen many boys like Clay, those who eagerly soaked in every detail of the prehistoric recreation, naming every giant and monster they saw in the mist. But Triumph could tell the boy was also worried. He kept looking back at his uncle as if he was wondering why his relative had become so distant and silent.

Triumph knew the answer. He didn't normally use his psychic powers to control his own employees, but in this case it had been the most expedient way to get the boy here. As diminished as Triumph's powers were, he could still easily bend most humans to his will.

The hidden observation platform was positioned two stories above the entrance of the Smithsonian Lounge, the most opulent restaurant in Lost World. The boy and his uncle drew close, then disappeared from sight as they entered the restaurant. Soon they would come up the elevator hidden behind a wall of the Lounge's exclusive private dining room.

Triumph heard the quiet hum of the elevator doors sliding open, then the startled gasp of the young boy.

"Oh my God!" Clay Ostrom cried. "It's him!"

Rex Triumph turned with a dancer's grace and looked into the astonished eyes of his young visitor. He knew he cut a dashing figure, dressed in a business suit as sleek as liquid midnight that accented his handsome, bronzed features and dark eyes. He smiled and lifted one eyebrow ever so slightly.

"I'm...My name is Clay Ostrom. Pleased to meet you, sir." Clay held out a tentative hand for Triumph to shake, as though he doubted his worthiness to touch such an imposing figure. Triumph understood. After all, he was a living legend in Las Vegas even though nobody knew his true secret.

Triumph clasped the child's hand. "A pleasure, Clay." He spared a momentary glance at the boy's uncle. "Ah. Thank you, Scott. You may go now."

Scott Ostrom offered a vacant smile, then shuffled back into the elevator like a sleepwalker. Clay's awed expression melted into worry as he watched his uncle depart.

"You needn't be concerned," Triumph said in his deep, refined voice. "Your uncle tells me you are a great fan of my Lost World, yes?"

The boy looked back at Triumph as his uncle disappeared behind the closing elevator doors. "Um...yes, sir. I am."

"This is a view few are privileged to see," Triumph said, sweeping his hand to take in the panorama of Lost World's forest. "What do you think?"

The boy took a few hesitant steps toward the balcony railing. "It's...incredible." Triumph watched Clay gaze out through the mist that wafted up from hidden generators into the nearly perfect representation of the world as it had been sixty-five million years before. Clay's eyes moved from the head of a great long-necked sauropod poking above the tree line, its jaws working as it seemed to munch on the sprawling cycad fronds, to a much closer and smaller creature.

"I've never seen that one before," Clay said.

Triumph gave a satisfied nod, glad that the boy had noticed the replica dinosaur clutching a thick tree trunk with its small claws.

"You cannot see it from anywhere else in Lost World," Triumph said, admiring the beautiful blue-and-red feathers that fanned from the tiny creature's wings and tail. Animatronic motors opened the animal's mouth to reveal neat rows of sharp teeth.

"It can't be an archaeopteryx," Clay said. "Those are from the Jurassic period. All your dinosaurs are from the late Cretaceous."

"Quite right," Triumph said, even more pleased. Guests like Clay were a rare treat. They appreciated the artistry and authentic details of Lost World, not just the spectacle and luxury. "That is avisaurus. A distant descendant of archaeopteryx. One of my favorites."

"It's pretty cool," Clay said, but his tone betrayed his underlying anxiety. "Sir...why'd you ask my uncle to bring me here? I mean, it's really great to meet you, but...um..." He trailed off, twitching like a mouse in a raptor's glare.

Triumph inhaled a deep breath, taking in both the boy's smell and psychic aura. His senses told him more than any mere human could perceive. A detailed profile of Clay's character unfolded in his mind—a smart boy, an outsider with few friends, the victim of many small injustices from his peers and his family. He detected

Clay's passionate love for worlds of the imagination, a romantic longing for enchantment and adventure, and...a secret very close to the surface. That was what Triumph had been hoping to find.

"Your uncle tells me that you saw a dragon at Hoover Dam last week," Triumph said.

"Oh," Clay said, rubbing his palms together, the tang of nervous sweat now infusing his scent. "That was... something I just made up to get attention. I know it was really a rogue drone like the news said."

Triumph tapped a finger on his chin. "To get attention, you say?"

"Yes, sir."

"You are a small boy for your age, Clay. You are intelligent and articulate. Bullies are drawn to you, are they not?"

The boy blushed. "Sometimes. Yeah."

"So why would a boy in your position want to call more attention to himself by claiming to see a dragon?"

Clay swallowed hard and looked away. "Well...I..."

"I know what really happened, Clay Ostrom," Triumph said. "You saw a dragon at Hoover Dam."

A nervous, fluttering laugh emerged from the boy's mouth. "But that's impossible, sir. There's no such thing."

Triumph made a soft tut-tut noise. "This puts me in a very peculiar situation. For if there are no dragons..." He let the thought hang in the air, then extended the force of his will toward Clay's mind.

He didn't need to dominate Clay, as he had with Scott Ostrom. Instead, he sent a vision more vivid than any daydream. He showed the boy Rex Triumph as he should be, in his true body and with his power fully restored. A phantom wind stirred the air as Triumph projected the image of mighty wings resplendent with plumage of blue and scarlet and gold, a long tail split into two feathery fans, killer claws an order of magnitude greater than those of a velociraptor, and glittering golden eyes filled with confidence.

He allowed the human child to behold the full glory of an adult dragon of the air.

Clay gasped and dropped to his knees, overwhelmed by the magnificence of the vision. Triumph withdrew his psychic touch, and the boy goggled in the wake of the marvel he'd just witnessed.

"If there are no dragons," Triumph repeated, "then what am I?"

"You're..." Clay wheezed. "You're a dragon too!"

"Ah. So you have met another."

The young human anxiously fiddled with his

glasses. "I'm not...I'm not supposed to tell anyone. She's a friend."

Triumph spread his hands in a placating gesture. "I mean your friend no harm. She and I are kin after all."

"You don't look like her," Clay said. "Her wings don't have feathers."

That detail told Triumph this other dragon was an Archon, the fire breed. They were the only other breed capable of flight, but their wings had membranes instead of feathers. As a species, they were more powerful than the dragons of air like Triumph. He would have to tread cautiously.

Triumph donned his most charming smile. "We are still both dragons. There are things I would like to know about your friend."

"Why ask me?" Clay said, peering suspiciously at Triumph now. "Why not go directly to her?"

Triumph sniffed, detecting a sharp sting of obstinacy in the boy's scent now. The child was both loyal to his friends and leery of Triumph.

Triumph was not entirely surprised. He was the darling of the Las Vegas media, but there was a darker undercurrent to his reputation. He'd used his powers to get ahead in the tough, sometimes violent world of the high-stakes city. Who knew what rumors this child had heard and what conclusions he'd drawn about Triumph's character?

Triumph tapped his chin and considered simply asserting psychic domination over Clay as he had with the boy's uncle. No mere child could resist him, no matter how willful. Yet Clay might be under the protection of this Archon. Triumph had no desire to needlessly provoke the other dragon.

But he needed to know the truth about the dragon. He needed to know she was the one he'd been waiting for all these years.

"This other dragon," Triumph began, "does she possess an enchanted stone?"

Clay's stunned gape was answer enough.

Triumph leaned forward until his eyes were level with the boy's. "Why has she not used it?"

Clay swayed as if he wanted to take a step back, but he stayed pinned in place by the intensity of Triumph's gaze. "She...We don't know what it's for. She doesn't remember."

"Ah," Triumph said, straightening to his full height again. "I see."

Clay wiped the sweat from his forehead. "How did you know about the stone?"

"Oh, I know a great deal," said Rex Triumph. "Bring

your dragon friend to me, Clay Ostrom, and I will tell her all she wishes to know about her Harbinger."

Chapter Thirteen

Games on Top of Games

Rose's insides felt like a tug-of-war between curiosity and fear. Rex Triumph wanted to meet. He claimed to be a dragon and promised he could tell them the secret of the Harbinger. He was offering them answers to all their questions.

Rose wondered if this was too good to be true.

She'd seen Rex Triumph a hundred times on TV, usually doing a crazy publicity stunt like jumping out of an airplane in his Elvis costume, crooning onstage with Wayne Newton, or letting magician David Copperfield saw him in half. His handsome face smiled across countless billboards, and some of his fans liked to call him the "King of Las Vegas." How could someone so much in the public eye be hiding a secret so huge?

But when Clay told her and Jade about his vision of Triumph in his true form, Jade was convinced that Triumph was really Six-Wing, a dragon of air. If Triumph was for real, Rose knew meeting him would be their best chance to solve the mystery of the Harbinger. She would go with Jade, Clay, and Mrs. Jersey this Sunday to meet the other dragon.

But Rex Triumph scared her.

She remembered her father talking to one of his friends who worked construction in Vegas about the billionaire casino mogul. Triumph had shown up out of the blue years before, hailing from Costa Rica and with a ton of money but no history of how he'd gotten it. "Things happen to people who get in Rex Triumph's way," her father had said. "Accidents. Misfortune. Creepy stuff. Scratch that glitzy surface, and you'll find a dangerous guy underneath."

Those words echoed through Rose's mind as she fidgeted her way through church that morning. Her keen-eyed father noticed something was up. "What's on your mind?" he asked.

"I'm just looking forward to showing Jade around Vegas," she said. She'd already told him about the planned trip, leaving out the part about dragons, of course.

He gave her one of his x-ray looks as they walked back to his truck. "When am I going to meet this new friend of yours?" He always made a point to know the people Rose spent her time with.

"Uh...soon, I hope," Rose said.

He grunted. "Looking forward to it." Then he cast an eye at the cloud-streaked sky. "We're in for nasty winds today. Make sure you dress for them."

Rose retreated to her room to change as soon as they got home, trading in her good Sunday clothes for her more familiar hoodie, cargo shorts, and pink-laced hiking boots. Thinking about the wind, she pulled her hair back with a ribbon, then paused in front of the mirror.

She still had on her earrings.

Rose didn't wear earrings very often, but her most precious possession was the pair of tiny diamond studs that had belonged to her mother. Her father disapproved of her wearing them any time except for church, but Rose had started to think of them as her good luck talisman and secretly wore them at other times, like when she had an important exam at school, or sometimes when she looked for rocks in the desert.

She felt like she always made her highest test scores and her best finds with the earrings on. Her father would've called that superstition, but she thought Mrs. Jersey might not dismiss it so easily. She ran her finger over one of the hard, brilliant stones, and decided today she needed all the luck she could get. She arranged her hair to cover her ears so her father wouldn't see them as she left.

* * *

When Jade set eyes on Las Vegas, it was love at first sight. Rose couldn't help but smile as she watched the dragon-girl leaning out the window of Mrs. Jersey's car, craning her neck as if she wanted to look at every dazzling, multicolored casino at once. Jade laughed in delight as she pointed out each one—the pirate ship of Treasure Island, the great fountains of the Bellagio, and the man-made volcano of the Mirage that blew piña colada–scented steam.

"So many people!" Jade said. "All so close together. Look at all the cars!"

"You ought to see it on New Year's," Clay said. "The whole Strip turns into one giant party."

The dragon-girl turned to Rose. "Is this a big city? Compared to other ones?"

"About medium sized, I guess," Rose said, then pointed to the city-within-a-city that was the New York, New York casino. "That's modeled after the biggest city in the nation."

"How many cities are there?"

"What, in the whole world?" Rose looked to Mrs. Jersey

for an answer, but the teacher was focused on the bumper-to-bumper traffic. Rose scratched her head. "I don't know."

Jade's head whipped around as another casino came into view. "Look!" she cried, pointing to a white castle-like resort that was the Excalibur. "It's the King Arthur place!" And with that, she threw open the door and ran into the street.

"Jade, no!" cried Mrs. Jersey.

Rose pressed herself against the window as she watched Jade weave her way toward the Excalibur through the creeping traffic. One taxi blared its horn at her, making her jump, and the dragon-girl whirled to answer with a braying shout almost identical to the car horn.

"We've got to help her!" Rose said.

Mrs. Jersey made a sharp move to the far-right lane, setting off even more blaring horns as she cut heedlessly across the tourist traffic. But she managed to thread her little car to the curb without getting into a wreck. "Go on," she said to Clay and Rose, waving them toward the sidewalk. "Get her out of the street. I'll meet you out front of the Excalibur."

"Come on, Clay!" Rose called.

The wind nearly slammed the door back into Rose's face as she forced her way out of the car. She and Clay sprinted together down the sidewalk. Jade had already gotten ahead by about a dozen cars, but she was easy to track by the sound of cars honking and her answering imitations. "Jade!" Rose shouted at the dragon-girl, who was grinning like a loon as angry drivers shouted out their windows. "Come here!"

Jade finally heard her, gave a little wave to the knot of stalled cars, and trotted cheerfully over to Rose and Clay.

Once her friend was safely on the sidewalk, Rose leaned over with her hands on her thighs and panted with relief. "We have got to teach you about traffic."

"I was learning," Jade said.

Rose shook her head and led the way to the Excalibur.

It didn't take them long to reach the medieval-style resort on foot, but with traffic, it would probably take Mrs. Jersey a lot longer. "The wind out here is brutal," Rose said when they reached the doors. "Let's go inside."

Rose wondered what Jade would make of the large purple dragon statue that greeted visitors to the hotel. Would she be amused, curious, or even insulted by the depiction? Jade barely gave the sculpture a second look. She ogled the elaborate chandeliers, then drifted around the lobby to examine whatever odd thing caught her interest. The bellhops gave her peculiar looks as she ran her fingernails along the smooth marble of the check-in counter.

"She's Dutch," Rose told them. They nodded politely.

Jade pointed at a gleaming suit of armor standing on display in the resort's promenade. "What's that?"

"It's called plate mail," Clay said. "Knights wore it for protection."

"So it's clothes?" Jade asked, studying the steel suit from every angle. "I've never seen anyone wearing this."

"It's not clothes really," Clay said. "It's armor for battle. And it's from a long time ago. Soldiers wear different kinds of armor today." A smile lit his face. "In fact, there's a modern version of scale mail with ceramic plates and silicon fibers called Dragon Skin armor."

This description immediately tickled Rose's imagination. Her artistic mind conjured up an image of what such armor might look like, a supple suit of overlapping scales that mimicked the graceful patterns of Jade's dragon hide. The image in her mind mixed with the vision of the medieval plate mail before her, with ornaments and joint guards to enhance the gleaming scale mesh. The military suit Clay mentioned probably looked more modern and practical, but Rose liked her imaginary version. She wished she had a sketchbook with her.

Jade finished her inspection of the armor and turned to Clay. "Where's King Arthur?"

Clay gave Rose a helpless look.

"He's not here today," Rose said. "Wanna see the casino instead?"

Jade nodded eagerly, and they moved to the edge of the cavernous gaming floor that dominated the lower level. Jade stared with wide eyes at the seemingly endless display of card tables, banks of television screens for sports gamblers, and slot machines with their never-ending chorus of bells and chimes. "What are they doing?" she asked, pointing at a cluster of tourists at the roulette table.

Rose tried her best to explain the difference between poker and blackjack and struggled to remember how the dice games worked.

"Where do the rules come from?" Jade asked.

"I don't know," Rose said. "People made up the rules a long time ago, and you learn them when you play with someone else."

"But most of these people come from far away," the dragon-girl said. "And they still know the same rules?"

"Pretty much," Rose said.

Jade shook her head, as if this was too much to take in. "What if a person wants to play by different rules?"

"You can't. Once you're in the casino, you have to play by their rules."

"So the casino can change the rules when they want?"

"The casino has to play by the rules too. I mean, the games work in their favor. That's how they make money. But if you win, they have to pay up. They can't change the games if they don't like it."

"Is it the same in all the other casinos?"

"Sure."

Jade's eyes swept the gambling floor. "How many people come here?"

"To Vegas? Tons. Millions every year."

Jade stared at her. "So you mean that millions of people come here. They use their dollars to play these games. They know they'll probably lose, but they agree to the rules anyway. And nobody can change the rules, not even the casinos."

"I guess it sounds pretty stupid," Rose said.

"It's amazing," Jade sighed in wonder.

"But dragons play games too," Clay said. "Like you did with me."

Jade spread her arms to take in the whole gambling floor. "Not like this. Two or three dragons may agree on the rules of a game, but the game comes to an end. Dragons make up new rules every time they start a new game. But with humans, your whole world plays games on top of games. I've been trying to understand humans since I met you, Rose. All the things I've seen—like traffic and money and laws—everything is a game. You have so many rules, and you all agree to them. Millions and millions of people, playing the same games." She beamed in delight. "Can't you see how amazing that is?"

"I've never thought about it that way," Rose said. She was in the middle of formulating a question about the world of dragons when her phone buzzed in her pocket. "Mrs. Jersey is waiting out front," she said as she read the text. "Come on."

They jogged toward the main entrance, Rose pulling a somewhat reluctant Jade along by the hand as the dragon-girl ogled the Camelot-style decorations along the way. Clay was out the main entry doors first, but Rose paused when she saw an elderly tourist struggling to make his way through the doors with his bulky luggage. She held the door open for the man and gave him a polite smile when he thanked her.

Jade stood staring with a peculiar look on her face.

"What?" Rose asked.

"Do you know him?" Jade said, pointing at the tourist.

"No."

"But you helped him anyway."

Rose shrugged. "Sure. He was having trouble with the door."

The dragon-girl's face was very still as she took this in.

"What's wrong?" Rose asked.

"Dragons don't do that," she said in a flat voice. "We don't just help someone we don't know." Now her brow creased with a troubled look. "Rex Triumph wants something from me."

Rose felt her stomach tighten. "What do you think he wants?"

"I don't know," Jade said. "I'm worried."

For someone who'd flown through the jet flow test and thought it was fun, that was really saying something. "You told me dragons aren't shy. They don't hide. But isn't Triumph hiding, sort of? He's got territory and all, but he's hiding the fact he's a dragon."

"Yes," Jade said in the same quiet, concerned voice. "I don't understand it."

Rose reached out and took Jade's hand, leading her gently toward the door and their waiting friends. "It's okay. We'll be fine as long as we stick together," she said and hoped it was true.

Chapter Fourteen

Dinner with Rex

As they entered Lost World, Rose held Jade's hand tight, but this time the dragon-girl showed no sign of wanting to wander off and take in the sights like she'd done at the Excalibur. She had a focused, almost grim set to her features as they made their way down the shopping promenade and arrived at the entrance to the Smithsonian Lounge, where Triumph had scheduled their meeting.

When Rose entered the opulent five-star restaurant, she had a fleeting wish that she'd stayed in her church clothes. Their party drew looks from the diners in their formal wear as the tuxedo-clad maître d' led them across the restaurant. They paused at a shadowy stretch of wall obscured behind marble columns. The maître d' touched a hidden switch, and the wall shifted and swung open.

"A secret door," Clay whispered. "Cool."

Rose felt too nervous to be impressed.

A long table of dark, rich wood stood at the center of the private room. It was set for dinner and surrounded by ornate chairs with velvet cushions of the deepest red, the woodwork ornamented with gold filigree. Huge glass display cases were set in the wall, each one containing a different dinosaur fossil on a velvet-covered pedestal.

But the opulence of the room paled next to its occupant. Rex Triumph greeted them dressed in fantastic gold silk robes embroidered with scarlet dragons, looking like a Chinese emperor.

"Welcome, my friends!" he said in his velvety Costa Rican accent. He beamed at them, his arms spread as if to embrace them all. The maître d' silently slid out the door and shut it behind him. "I am so pleased you could make it."

He saluted them one by one, first giving Clay's hand a robust shake. "Ah, my young friend. Thank you for arranging this."

Clay's voice came out squeaky. "Sure...no problem, sir."

Triumph moved on. "You must be Mrs. Doris Jersey. An honor to meet you in person." He made a sweeping bow and kissed her fingers.

Mrs. Jersey looked small and frumpy next to the billionaire in his glorious imperial robes, but she didn't seem at all intimidated and answered in a polite but cool voice. "Kind of you to invite us."

He swept his way to Rose next, filling her vision like a silk sunrise. His dark eyes glittered as he inspected her. She resisted a sudden urge to shrink back against the wall. Meeting a celebrity was intimidating enough, and she knew Triumph was much more than he appeared. "Miss Rose Gallagher. Clay spoke of your courage. I am humbled to be in your presence."

He had an awfully strange way of being humble. "Hi" was all she could think to say.

He shook her hand with a gentle but strong grip, then pivoted to the last member of their group. "Jade, as you are called. My lady, I welcome you to my dwellings with the greatest reverence. If there is anything you desire, please do not hesitate to ask."

Jade said nothing, merely studied the spectacle of a man before her with calm, detached eyes. Only when she moved her hand to rest against the pocket where she kept the Harbinger did Jade betray any emotion.

Triumph motioned them to the cushioned chairs.

Rose settled in the seat next to Jade and watched Rex Triumph with sharp suspicion.

"Would you care to order an appetizer?" their host asked. "Feel free to request anything on the menu. It is my treat. Perhaps the wine list, Mrs. Jersey?"

"I would prefer to get down to business, if you please," Mrs. Jersey replied. She gave him a tart little smile. "We appreciate your hospitality, but for the moment I think it's best we decline your offer."

Rose tightened her hands into fists under the table. Since they didn't know what Triumph might do, they had agreed the safest approach was to be polite but firm. In stories about spirits and faeries, most gifts came with strings of obligation attached, and consuming the food and drink of a supernatural being could put you in its power.

They would accept nothing from Rex Triumph until they knew more about his motives. In the meantime, Mrs. Jersey would do the talking. Rose glanced at the teacher's lined and gentle features, and felt comforted by the cool resolve she saw in those eyes. Mrs. Jersey wasn't awed by Rex Triumph's flamboyant wealth and power.

Triumph steepled his fingers, studying the teacher. "Ah." He let out a regretful sigh. "You are one of those sorts, aren't you?"

Mrs. Jersey raised an eyebrow. "What sort might that be, Mr. Triumph?"

"Someone who thinks a paltry study of folklore makes one an expert on magic," he said. "I was hoping for a civilized conversation. But I can see that won't be possible."

Mrs. Jersey said calmly, "We can be as civilized as you wish—"

"*Go to sleep,*" Triumph commanded.

He gave a dismissive wave of his hand that took in the whole room, and suddenly Rose's vision turned blurry. She wobbled in her chair and reached out to clutch Jade for support. The moment she touched her friend's arm, her dizziness vanished. She sat up sharply, wondering what had just happened.

Mrs. Jersey and Clay slumped in their seats, sound asleep.

"What did you do?" Rose cried. She shot to her feet, and Jade stood beside her.

For a moment, she was sure that Rex Triumph looked startled. But then his mask of casual geniality fell back into place. "That is much better," he said.

"Why did you do that?" Rose shouted, glaring at Triumph with undisguised fury. She moved to Mrs. Jersey's side, hoping to shake the teacher awake.

"Your friends are simply sleeping," Triumph said. "I advise you not to wake them."

Rose froze. "Why not?"

"Because I do not want to talk to them. I wish to speak only to Jade."

Rose turned to Jade. The dragon-girl scowled. "That was rude," Jade said. "They're with me."

Triumph bowed his head in a gesture that was almost subservient. "My apologies, Lady. But this is my home, and I choose with whom I speak."

"You invited them," Jade said.

"I invited you. They simply came along."

Jade narrowed her eyes. "You're upsetting me."

Triumph spread his hands before her. "I mean no offense. I would never intentionally anger an Archon such as you. But the matters we must speak of are for the ears of dragons, not humans."

Rose moved closer to Jade's side. "I'm not leaving!" she said.

Jade nodded. "Rose stays with me."

Triumph bowed graciously. "Very well."

"I want you to wake up our friends too," Rose said, planting her feet.

"I am sure your Mrs. Jersey is a lovely person, but I am a busy man, and I do not have time to deal with her scrutinizing my every word. You can explain things to her later." He turned and moved to the far wall. He touched an invisible switch, and one of the ornate panels slid aside to reveal a narrow passage. Rose could make out the outline of an elevator door down the hall.

"Are you coming?" he asked. "Or do you wish to remain ignorant about the Harbinger?"

Rose turned to Jade. "Can you make him wake up Mrs. Jersey and Clay since you're one of those Archon dragons?"

Jade frowned and whispered, "I'm the fire breed, the highest order of dragons. But he's older and we're in his home." She shook her head. "Let's go with him. If he starts any more trouble, I can deal with him."

Rose took a deep breath and gathered up her backpack. She gave one furtive last look at Mrs. Jersey and tightened her grip on Jade's hand. "All right," she said. "I'm ready."

Chapter Fifteen

The Story of Dragons

The private elevator ascended so smoothly that Rose could barely feel it moving. She pressed herself against the wall of the car, clutching Jade's hand as she glared at their gold-robed host. They rode in silence until the doors finally opened with a soft chime.

"My home," Triumph said. "Come. Make yourselves comfortable, my friends."

Rose had expected a lavish luxury suite like she'd seen in countless Vegas advertisements. Rex Triumph's penthouse made those places seem as cramped as cupboards. With its vaulted ceilings and spacious layout, it was practically a mansion. They followed Triumph in, Rose's sneakers squeaking against the gleaming tile.

Though he'd given himself plenty of space, Triumph hardly had any furniture. A large desk stood on a raised dais, a staircase led up to a lounge area with couches and comfortable chairs, and a few side tables and bookshelves were placed here and there, but otherwise the vast apartment consisted of empty space.

"What do you think of the view?" Triumph asked, sweeping his hand toward the room's towering glass windows. From this vantage, an observer could look out across the city and onto the rugged mountains rising above the Nevada desert. The winds had blown away the smog that normally smothered the valley, and the scenery stood out with diamond clarity. The sky was deepening from blue to purple as the sun set, and along the Strip, the casinos glowed in a sea of multicolored splendor.

"It's great," Rose said. "So what did you want to tell us?"

"So impatient!" the billionaire said, laughing. "But of course, you are very young."

"So?" she shot back. "How old are you, anyway?"

"Sixty-five million years old, give or take."

She gaped at him. All the stories about dragons described them as being long-lived or even immortal, but Rose could hardly believe him. "That was the end of the Mesozoic," she said. "The great extinction, when the dinosaurs died out. You were there sixty-five million years ago?"

"Quite right."

She turned to Jade, who looked just as mystified. "Nobody's that old," the dragon-girl said.

Triumph chuckled. "Perhaps I should tell you our story—the story of dragons. Then it will become clear."

"I hope so," Rose said shakily.

"Human beings consider themselves to be the first intelligent civilization this planet has ever produced," Triumph began. "In fact, they are the second. The first was my kind: dragons. We ascended—or evolved, if you like—from the beings you call dinosaurs, when humanity's ancestors were no more than rats scuttling beneath the feet of giants."

"If that's true, why haven't we ever found dragon bones?" Rose asked. Her father had taught her about fossils as well as stones. "Or are some dinosaurs really..." She remembered reading a *National Geographic* article that suggested some ancient people might have believed dinosaur bones belonged to dragons.

"We do not become fossils," Triumph said. "When it is time for a dragon to leave this world, he does not simply rot in the muck like some dumb beast. We leave this world to enter the realm of death when we choose, body and soul alike."

"But nobody's ever found ruins of your civilization from that long ago."

"Because you think of civilization in human terms," Triumph said. He pointed out the window toward the Vegas skyline. "Buildings and roads. Pottery. Tombs. Statues. All these things you think of as civilization, but that is not the way of dragons. Our monuments were forged from our will and built in poetry and song! Our cathedrals were the sky and sea! Trees and valleys, the wind and the water, the living creatures around us, the magnificence of our very bodies...these were where we focused our craft. Of course humans never recognized the evidence. How could you?"

"I think humans are clever," Jade said.

"Clever," Triumph said. "Yes. That is a good word for them. Cunning with their tools and their devices. I will give them that, at least. I have harnessed the tools of humankind to build this great casino, to remind me of our bygone age. You do know what occurred sixty-five million years ago, at the end of the time you call the Mesozoic Era, yes?"

Rose frowned in thought. "A comet hit the earth and wiped out the dinosaurs. We've found evidence, like iridium deposits that came from space and the Chicxulub impact crater in Mexico where the comet hit."

"This is only partially correct," Triumph said. "There were, in fact, two comets that struck our world."

"Two?"

"Horrors from the sky," Triumph said in a haunted voice. "They plunged with wrath from the heavens and brought disaster to the world. The first that struck was the smaller of the two. It hurled clouds of dust into the sky that lasted for years, devastating the land like a hundred erupting volcanoes. That comet was the Harbinger."

Rose gasped. "The Harbinger! Jade's stone? That's where it came from?"

Triumph nodded. "Indeed. We called the comet itself the *Harbinger*, or the equivalent in our tongue. The stone Lady Jade carries might be more properly named *Of the Harbinger*, but let us not quibble. The greatest tektite formed by that catastrophe became the vessel for immense power...the power to save dragonkind from the second, much greater impact that wiped out the dinosaurs and cast the world into darkness."

"How?" Rose asked. "What did the dragons do?"

"We slept."

Jade let out a small gasp. "Yes...yes! Now I remember!"

Rose shook her head. "I don't understand. You hibernated through the disaster?"

"Not as you are thinking," Triumph said. "Ours was

an enchanted sleep that took us to the edge of death itself."

"But where are your bodies?" Rose asked. "If there are so many sleeping dragons around, wouldn't somebody have uncovered one of them?"

"You have seen Jade change her shape. For this sleep, we changed as well, merging our bodies with the elements so they would not be destroyed by the cataclysm. Now we are all around you," Triumph swept a hand toward the window, taking in the panorama of the Nevada desert under the setting sun.

"Look in the clouds! Do you not sometimes see dragons dancing in the air? There, along that ridge of stone! A dragon in repose, its neck stretched out along the rise. Flowing in the rivers, in the oceans, in the air and stone and fire. We are everywhere you look, if you have but eyes to see."

Rose couldn't wrap her head around the idea. She turned to Jade. "Does he mean a cloud shape can be a sleeping dragon? What happens when the cloud evaporates?"

Jade gazed dreamily at the clouds. "We sleep in the repeating forms of the world. A dragon that sleeps as a cloud might be that cloud, right there. See? Then it disperses, and he's gone until his cloud comes again.

He slips back into deeper sleep."

Rose pursed her lips. "But that cloud won't ever appear again, not exactly the same as it was."

Jade's face split into a wide grin, as if Rose had just told a truly excellent joke. "Nothing's ever exactly the same as it was."

Rose opened her mouth, then closed it and considered. A dragon's body became a rock formation, a cloud, a gust of wind, or a breaking wave. These forms were always changing—even the seemingly solid ones, like rocks. But was Rose's own body any different? She aged; she grew. She got wounds that healed and left scars. She ate and drank different things that became part of her. Every breath she took cycled through a new and unique portion of air. Yet her mind and soul somehow stayed attached to her ever-changing physical form.

Rose thought it must be the same for the sleeping dragons...if more extreme.

She shook her head—this was a lot to take in. She turned to Triumph. "So are most dragons still asleep?"

"We are all asleep," Triumph said. "What you see before you is a dream."

Rose suppressed a sudden urge to reach out and poke him. "You're not real?"

He chuckled. "Sometimes our sleep is deeper. There are times when we dream of the world you inhabit, the realm of matter and substance. At such times, our dreaming selves can walk in the world. We are shades...phantoms."

"You seem pretty solid," Rose said.

"Do I?" He reached up and tore a strip of silk from his robe. "Hold out your hand."

But when he dropped the strip of cloth, it never landed in her hand. It melted out of sight as it left his grasp, vanishing into nothingness. She felt only a soft rush of air on her fingers, like the breath from a kitten.

Rose looked at him wide-eyed. Triumph grinned back at her. "Phantoms or not, we are still dragons. Even our dreams can take on substance. Dragons have walked among humankind for all of your brief existence. Many of your legends of gods and heroes and monsters are really about dragons like myself who walked as living dreams in your world." He smiled, his voice taking on a nostalgic tone. "Centuries ago, I was worshipped for a time by the people called the Olmec. I appeared to them as a dragon, not a man."

Rose recalled images from her mother's books of other feathered Mesoamerican dragons—the Aztec Quetzalcoatl and the Mayan Kukulcan—and wondered if all those myths really traced back to Rex Triumph.

Triumph's wistful expression grew more somber. "Our dreams may last years or seconds, but they always end. In time, deeper sleep takes us, and we fade from the world to return to the borderlands between dream and death. To wait for the Awakening."

Rose suddenly became aware of the warmth of Jade's hand in her own. She turned to look at her friend. "Does that mean that you're just a dream too? Like him?"

Jade fixed her brilliant-green gaze on Rose. "No. I am the first."

"Indeed," Triumph said. "I was not accurate to say we are all asleep, Miss Gallagher. Lady Jade is awake. After sixty-five million years, she is the first to awake."

Hundreds of questions swirled through Rose's mind. The first to pop out was: "Why did it take so long?"

Triumph's expression changed. For a moment, he looked confused, and even hurt. His self-assured smile quickly covered it, but Rose knew what she'd seen. "A good question. It does seem like you took your time returning to us, Lady Jade. Have you ever dreamed yourself into the world?"

The dragon-girl's eyes grew distant. "Never. My last memory was of wrapping myself around the Harbinger and descending into sleep. My body became the heat of sunlight on sand. I had no idea I'd been asleep so long." She turned to Rose and smiled. "But I did dream of you."

Rose blinked. "You did? When?"

"Many times. When you walked in the desert or rode your horse close to the place where I slept. I could feel you when I dreamed. You called to me."

"How?" Rose asked. "I didn't even know you were there."

Jade smiled. "Some part of you did."

"I-I think you're right," Rose said. In all her solitary trips into the desert, she'd never felt like she was alone. When she'd felt the loneliest—like after an argument with her father—the best remedy had always been to walk by herself into the desert. Had she somehow sensed she had a kindred spirit there? "So I helped wake you up?"

Jade nodded. "I think so. I was so happy to wake up. So much is unfamiliar. But I don't know how much has really changed and how much I've forgotten."

Rose felt a deeper appreciation for Jade's memory problems. After spending millions of years in an enchanted sleep, it wasn't surprising Jade needed a while to get her brains back in order.

"Very touching, of course," Triumph said. "Yet

surely you now recall your true purpose and that of the Harbinger, Lady Jade."

"I'm beginning to remember," she said. "But why would it take so many years for me to wake up?" She frowned, her lips pressed tight in concentration.

"Ah, truly a mystery!" the billionaire said, in a tone that suggested it was a mystery he had no desire to explore. "But now you must fulfill your great task."

"To use the Harbinger to awaken the dragons," Jade said.

Rose felt a shiver run down her spine. "Why can't they just wake up by themselves?"

Triumph let out a hollow laugh. "It is not so easy, Miss Gallagher. We sleep mingled with fire and wind, earth and water. Do you see? We needed a tool to draw us back from a slumber that deep, so close to death. And so the queen of the Archons, mightiest of all dragons, created the Harbinger. She gave it to her daughter to use for our awakening." He cocked his head, looking slightly puzzled. "And she chose her youngest daughter at that."

"Yes," Jade said, taking the Harbinger from her pocket. She held the tektite in both hands and examined it, peering into its luminous depths. "My mother trusted it to me. She said I was the sweetest of her children."

The memory brought a surprised smile to her face, but then her expression darkened. "When Mother gave me the stone, I remember seeing the comet in the sky, the end of the world rushing toward us. It glowed brighter than the moon. To survive, we had to sleep."

"And now you're supposed to bring back all the dragons that were alive then?" Rose asked, her mind reeling at the thought of a world populated by dragons. "What about human beings?"

Silence filled the vast chambers of Rex Triumph's suite.

Rose's voice trembled as she spoke. "If you wake up dragons, people are going to panic. It'll be...I don't know what will happen. People will be terrified."

"We have the right to exist," Triumph said. "This was our world before you arrived."

"But there are billions of people in the world now, and they have a right to exist too. Don't you think so, Jade?"

"Of course," Jade said.

She replied with such certainty that it seemed to throw Rex Triumph off his stride. He closed his mouth, swallowing whatever he had been about to say, then smiled. "Yes, it is as you say. This is the time of humans now, and we dragons will have to adjust to that. But we are very adaptable, are we not?"

"That's true," Jade said.

"You mean you can change your shape to blend in," Rose said. It would still be a huge disruption, so many people showing up with powers like Triumph and Jade, though maybe less of a shock than thousands or even millions of dragons suddenly appearing.

"That is one option," Triumph said. Rose could see him studying Jade's reactions and had the impression he was choosing his words with care now.

"It's still going to cause chaos," Rose said. "A lot of dragons may be like Jade when she first woke up. They won't know the language or laws or anything. If they fly around and breathe fire at people, it's gonna be bad." She gripped Jade's hand. "I don't know if humans are ready to share the world with real dragons."

Rose saw sympathy in Jade's green eyes but also a terrible resolve Rose had never imagined.

"These are my people, Rose," Jade said.

Rose's mouth went dry. "But—"

"I was given a duty," she continued. "A sacred task. Dragons have been waiting for me for so long. I can't fail them."

"Well spoken, Lady Jade," Triumph said.

Rose didn't know what she could say to talk her friend out of using the Harbinger. She wished with all her heart that Mrs. Jersey were here or even Clay. She needed someone else to speak for humanity as these dragons decided the fate of the world.

Jade returned her gaze to the tektite. "I...I'm not sure what to do."

Rose held her breath, hope kindling inside her.

"The Harbinger has been so stubborn," Jade said. "I'm not sure if I can make it work."

As Rose's heart plummeted, Rex Triumph's smile spread wide across his handsome face. "Then you need to test it," he said. "Fortunately, a most willing volunteer stands before you."

Chapter Sixteen

Triumphant Awakening

By the time they got out of the limousine, Rose could feel her heart galloping like a thoroughbred in her chest. She had a thousand things she wanted to say, but it felt as if a clamp around her throat keeping her from speaking. She wanted to make Jade look at her, to take her hand and plead for her to leave the dragons asleep. But Jade was separated from her by the gulf of Triumph's luxurious car. The dragon-girl held the tektite in both hands, peering into its cloudy green depths. She barely seemed to notice Rose.

In her mind's eye, Rose saw hundreds of dragons rising over the skies of Las Vegas, the neon lights beaming up into their dark wings as they wheeled and swooped over the city. Windows trembled as jet fighters hurtled through the atmosphere faster than sound, lacerating the air with their gunfire. Dragons shrieked in rage and spat flames; missiles crisscrossed and blossomed into red plumes of destruction. Rose didn't care who would win in such a battle. If humans and dragons went to war, she didn't think there would be any real winners.

But she didn't know what she could say to Jade. She tried to imagine if the fate of billions of sleeping humans rested in her hands. Her father, her friends, everyone she'd ever met...She wouldn't be able to just leave them trapped like the characters in Sleeping Beauty.

Her legs shook as she climbed out of Rex Triumph's sleek limousine. The billionaire told the driver they wouldn't need him for the rest of the night, but Rose barely heard. She hunched her back against the storm, shielding her eyes from the swirling sand blown in from the desert.

"Follow me," Triumph said, raising his voice above the rush of the wind. His silken robes whipped and billowed around him, rippling like an ocean of liquid gold. He looked so real, even though she knew now he was only the dream-ghost of a slumbering dragon.

Jade fell in behind him and Rose followed.

They had arrived at the construction site for the Triumphant, the new mega-casino Triumph was building. Supposedly it was going to be the biggest ever built. Rose remembered her father's raspy laugh when construction of the mega-casino was announced. He said it might be almost as big as Rex Triumph's ego.

A twelve-foot-tall barricade encircled the entire site to keep tourists out and to shield the surrounding area from the dust and noise of construction. The wooden wall sported a thick layer of advertising posters for stage magicians and circus shows. One tore loose as they passed, fluttering down the street like a panicked bat. Triumph led them to the padlocked gate and produced a ring of keys from his sleeve. Rose wondered if they were real keys or if he had dreamed them into existence. Whichever they were, they worked just fine. He ushered the girls into the site and snapped the lock shut behind them.

The barrier provided some shelter from the wind. Rose looked around at the parked construction equipment, piles of rebar, and tools, barrels, and crates. Nobody else was here—nobody she could turn to for help.

Rex Triumph led them deeper into the site along packed dirt paths, until Rose could make out the sound of rushing water ahead of them. As they came around the side of a massive yellow bulldozer, she saw the source. Standing there in all its glory among the steel and machinery was a stunningly beautiful waterfall.

It looked so incongruous amid the unsightly sprawl of half-built casino that it seemed like a visitor from another world.

Rose tilted her head as the fine mist from the waterfall washed over her and she inhaled the sweet fragrance of wet earth and flowers from a distant land. She realized it was all real, not like the artificial forest in Lost World.

"I can feel a presence here," Jade said.

"Yes," Triumph said. "Even humans can feel that there is something special about places like this, though they never know what it is. They sometimes even worship such places as sacred. But none realize that what they are feeling is the power of a sleeping dragon." He gestured to the waterfall. "And that, Lady Jade, is where I sleep."

"You're the waterfall?" Rose asked, feeling like she had to force each word out past a dam in her throat.

Triumph raised an eyebrow, looking mildly surprised. "Just so, Rose Gallagher. As long as this rushing water holds to this essential shape and formation, I am able to maintain myself in this dream, you see. Should the land change, I would eventually slip back into sleep until a waterfall like this one came again. Some dragons are so deep in dreams that even the Harbinger may not be able to wake them. But there are many like myself who are, as you might say, closer to the surface."

He folded his hands behind his back and regarded the rushing water. "I took great pains to have this formation brought from Costa Rica to here, where I could make sure it stayed intact. Developers were looking at the land, and they might have diverted my river. Now I need not worry about such things." He turned and made a sweeping bow to Jade. "For here you are! And now, my good lady, I ask you to awaken me."

"Just you?" Rose asked, and turned to Jade. She still felt a stifling feeling every time she tried to speak, but her desperation gave her voice strength. "If you use the Harbinger, won't it wake up all the dragons?"

Jade stayed silent for several long moments, staring into the Harbinger. "Since my memory came back, the Harbinger is starting to speak to me again," she said. "I think it will do as I wish."

"It's too big a risk!" Rose said, and for a moment she saw a flicker of doubt on Jade's face. "Don't do it!"

Rex Triumph threw himself at Jade's feet, bowing like a vassal before a queen. "Please, my lady! I beg this boon of you. It has been such a very long time. You felt it, did you not? When you awoke, you felt the joy of sunlight upon your body, the thrill of filling your lungs with the air of the living world. You remember, don't you?"

Jade nodded. "Yes."

"I yearn for it!" He clutched her arm. "I long to rise into the air on my real wings. Please, Lady Jade. Do not deny me! Do not condemn me to this half-life!"

Even through her fear, the anguish in Rex Triumph's voice struck at Rose's heart. She knew the die was cast.

Jade smiled at the man kneeling before her. "Yes," she said. "Stand back, Rose."

Rose edged away from the waterfall, taking shelter near a large stack of I-beams.

The air shimmered, and suddenly the great sinewy bulk of Jade's dragon form filled the half-built plaza. She stretched her wings to their full span and let out a little rumble of pleasure as if enjoying the feel of being back in her true shape.

Triumph gazed at her with rapturous delight. "Ah, yes! Call to me now in our true tongue. Call me by my name, and I shall respond!"

Jade gathered herself on her haunches, then bounded aloft. The wind caught her as she cleared the sheltering earthworks, throwing off her balance. Steadying herself with the counterweight of her tail, she hovered before the waterfall. A green-gold radiance shone from the Harbinger, intensifying with every stroke of Jade's wings.

This time, the air didn't just shimmer as Jade worked her magic—it churned. Rose gripped the steel of the beams as the world lurched around her, disoriented almost to the point of sickness by the sudden surge of invisible energy that warped her every perception. The ground bucked beneath her like a startled colt, while the frame of the Triumphant twisted crazily overhead. She collapsed to her knees and tried not to faint.

Jade let out a roar.

The part of Rose's mind that understood the language of dragons recognized this as the true name of the dream figure in the golden robes, his dragon name. Her mind had no direct translation, so she simply thought: *Rex Triumph.*

Rose looked at Triumph, who stood beneath Jade's hovering form with his arms upraised. Was he singing? Screaming? Rose couldn't tell. The distortion of the magical forces made it impossible to see him clearly.

Jade raised her voice again in a sharp keen of command that Rose's mind had no trouble interpreting: *Come forth!*

The Harbinger flared with eye-searing brilliance.

The waterfall twisted, water and mist rising in a

furious tornado-like spiral. The frothing mass shot into the air, trembled and coiled in on itself, and gathered into a great spinning oval that hung suspended for a split second. Then the churning egg of foam and vapor flew apart with a thunderclap, and Rose turned her head to shield her face against the sudden violent spray from the explosion.

When she turned back, she saw the second dragon.

Rex Triumph was so unlike Jade that Rose found it hard to believe they were both dragons. Where Jade's wings had delicately patterned membrane, Triumph's sported vast feathers alive with iridescent blue, gold, and scarlet. These feathers not only fanned out from the elongated forelegs that formed his wings, but tufts of brilliant plumage also adorned his rear legs, and his tail split into two feathery fans of shimmering blue-green. The arrangement made it look like he had six wings instead of two. The scales over the rest of his body shone like a mosaic of polished turquoise and amethyst, with a burnished golden hue on the armor plates on his underside. Next to the green Jade, he was a living riot of color.

He was also much bigger. Jade might have been the superior breed, but the long, lean form of Rex Triumph dwarfed her. His wingspan stretched twice as wide as

Jade's, and his back legs sported velociraptor-like killer claws as long as scimitars.

The dragon Triumph threw his great head back and let out a fluting cry of exultation. Rose pressed her palms to her ears. She thought her skull might crack with the force of the piercing sound.

With an excited lash of his feathered tail that scattered a stack of construction tools and supply barrels, Triumph gathered himself to leap. He sprang up to join Jade in the air. Where the green dragon fought the whipping wind to keep her position, Triumph rode the currents up through the girders with effortless grace, swift and sure as a dancer.

Triumph circled the hovering Jade, uttering a bewildering series of sharp clicks and musical warbles. Rose could barely keep up with the torrent of information. Translating Jade's voice was hard enough on Rose's brain, but trying to follow the conversation of two dragons threatened to overwhelm her.

He wanted Jade to use the Harbinger to wake the rest of the dragons. Images flashed through Rose's mind of armored wingless dragons bursting forth from the earth, serpentine dragons twisting their way free of rivers, six-winged dragons like Triumph emerging from clouds. She saw images of Jade's cousins as well, mighty Archon dragons of every hue materializing from the smoke of forest fires, from baking rocks in the desert, from the vents of steam erupting from geysers. Dragons of all shapes and sizes filled her mind's eye, swirling through her imagination as Rex Triumph pleaded his case.

What about the humans? Jade asked him.

Rose wanted to scream to her and tell her not to listen to Triumph. Humans would fight back if dragons invaded their world. But again she felt like an invisible hand was squeezing her voice box, and she couldn't force out a sound. A blast of wind caught one of the barrels that Rex Triumph's tail had dislodged and sent it toppling, spewing forth a cloud of black powder. The billowing cloud enveloped Rose, blinding her and filling her mouth with graphite powder. She fell to her knees, hacking violently to clear the fine carbon dust from her lungs.

Jade and Triumph sang to each other overhead in the tongue of dragons, but Rose couldn't follow, couldn't breathe...

She looked up with blurry eyes, rubbing desperately to try to clear her vision. A flick of a glossy green tail caught a stray beam of light from the city below, and then nothing. The dragons were gone.

Chapter Seventeen

Bound by Blood

Rose slumped against a stack of sandbags and wept in convulsive waves of despair that threatened to choke her. Their meeting with Rex Triumph had gone worse than she'd ever imagined. Triumph had scattered their defenses to the wind. He had easily defeated Mrs. Jersey, turned Jade to his side, and rendered Rose powerless to stop what was happening. Bitter, helpless tears smudged the graphite across Rose's cheeks. She wished with all her heart that they'd never agreed to see Triumph. She wished she'd missed her grab at the Harbinger, let it tumble into the surging waters beneath the Hoover Dam. Her dad had been right to throw it away.

The thought of her father sent a jolt through her nerves, a mixture of guilt and desperate hope. She should've told him about Jade from the start. She fumbled for her phone, pausing to rub at the grimy mucus under her nose with the back of her sleeve. The construction site was a bad place to call from—only one tiny bar flickered on her screen. She looked up at the steel framework of the unfinished hotel, tons of exposed metal interfering with her connection. With a deep, shuddering breath, she dialed her father and pressed the phone against her ear.

He picked up on the third ring. "Rose?"

Between the feeble connection and the noise of the waterfall, she could barely hear him. Cupping her hands over the phone, she shouted, "I'm in trouble, Dad!"

She heard something from the other end, but she couldn't make out his words. She hoped he'd be able to understand her. "I'm at the construction site for the Triumphant. Triumph...Jade...What they're going to do...It'll be a disaster! I couldn't do anything about it. Now I'm all alone..."

She was crying again and didn't know what she was saying. "Mrs. Jersey is unconscious...Triumph did it... He took me in the limo, and now he's going to..."

She couldn't say "awaken the dragons" to her father. He wouldn't know what she meant. She needed something he could understand.

"A bomb!" she lied. "It's a bomb or something...He's going to destroy everything!" That didn't really make sense, but at least it was something her father could grasp. "The construction site, Dad! Please come...Are you there? Can you hear me?"

She pulled her phone away to look at the screen. The call had ended. The signal was lost, and she only had a little bit of battery life left.

Rose folded her knees to her chest and rocked herself back and forth, feeling small and helpless in the face of the looming catastrophe of a dragon-human war. She couldn't remember ever feeling so wretched. The only memory that came close was when her mother died. She remembered how she'd wept that day, and seeing the tears running down her father's rugged face as he held her. His tears had been almost as shocking to her six-year-old mind as the news of her mother's accident. The idea that something could make her father cry had never occurred to her before that day.

Her dad would come, she told herself. He'd hold her and wipe her tears away like he had that day, and she'd tell him everything, and he'd...

He'd do what?

Nothing. There was nothing he could do. He was more than an hour's drive away, and even when he got to her, there was nothing he could do against the likes of Rex Triumph. Suddenly she despised herself, sitting there and bawling like a baby, hoping her father would come and fix everything.

Rose got to her feet.

She had to get to Jade. Rose knew that her friend still doubted whether she was doing the right thing. What she didn't know was how long it would take Jade and Triumph to use the Harbinger in the way Triumph intended. Rose might already be too late, but she couldn't think about that possibility. She had to believe she still had a chance to avert disaster.

Lost World was only a few blocks away. She could make it in ten minutes.

But when she reached the gate to the Triumphant, she realized Triumph had locked it behind them when they had arrived. She looked around at the construction site's twelve-foot-high wooden wall. She stared up at the barrier, her heart teetering between despair and rage. She gave the wall a hard kick, then looked around for something she could climb.

She didn't see anything as helpful as a ladder, but she did spy a stack of collapsible orange-and-white barricades leaning against the wall. They might do the trick. She hauled one out of the stack, positioning it so it seemed secure against the wall. The slats weren't meant to hold a person's weight, but she was light. She clambered up until she stood on the top of her makeshift ladder.

The top of the wall was still at least three feet out of reach. With a frustrated growl, she tried to jump and catch the upper rim of the wall—but came up short of her target. Flailing for balance as she fell, she felt her right hand snag on the protruding end of a nail. She landed hard, skinning her knees on the gravel-strewn concrete.

Rose bolted to her feet with a scream of rage and slammed her fists against the boards. "Somebody let me out of here! Hey! I'm trapped in here! *Let me out!*"

She carried on like that for a while, swearing so furiously that her father would've grounded her for a month if he'd heard her. She hit the wall over and over again until drops of scarlet flew from her injured hand. Nobody called out from the other side. Even if someone had walked by, she doubted anybody could hear her over the wind and the traffic.

The pain and the blood finally forced her to stop. The nail had left a ragged trail across her thumb and part of her palm. It had reopened the cut she'd made herself in Keyhole Canyon, when she and Jade had stood in a circle while Mrs. Jersey pounded her drum under the crystal-blue desert sky.

Rose put her thumb to her mouth and a memory stirred within her.

Jade wasn't just Rose's friend—she was her blood-sister. In a way, they could read each other's minds. That was how they shared their languages. Rose had felt Jade fish out information from her own memory. Rose realized she did the same thing every time she translated the speech of dragons, reaching by instinct into Jade's mind to find a meaning for what her ears heard.

Maybe their connection didn't have to be just instinct. Maybe she could reach Jade consciously.

Rose closed her eyes and thought with all her might. *Jade!*

Sweat trickled down her face. She hunched over, bearing down like she was trying to lift an anvil with only her thoughts.

Jade!

The muscles in her jaw clenched and she balled her fists, squinting her eyes shut. She tried to focus all her energy on picturing the dragon, putting as much mental effort as she could into producing a psychic shout that would reach her friend's mind.

Jade! JADE!

Nothing happened.

She wondered what she'd feel if she were able to reach Jade. Would she hear the dragon-girl's voice speaking in her head, like a telephone on the inside of her skull?

Rose was having a hard time concentrating. Her fear kept getting in the way. It blared at her like an alarm, telling her time was running out and tossed up unwanted images of dragons and humans battling in the Las Vegas skies. The pain in her hand also distracted her, and some practical part of her warned of infection if she didn't clean the wound out soon.

At least she had clean water available. Rose headed back to the fountain.

The feeling in the air around the waterfall was strangely different. The fountain was still a thing of beauty, but Rose could tell something had shifted now that the spirit of the sleeping dragon had departed. Before, she had sensed a charge permeating the atmosphere. It had been powerful but so subtle that she only noticed it now that it was gone.

Cold stung her injured hand as she plunged it into the water. She drew in a sharp gasp at the shock, but it felt good to cleanse the wound. Her blood spread out and mingled with the churning water, and she rubbed carefully at the cut to wash out any grit that might have found its way under her skin. As she fished out her first aid kit from her backpack, she tried to figure out a way to escape the construction site. A pang shot through her as she remembered the last time she'd used the kit when they were in Keyhole Canyon.

Rose froze, suddenly struck by a realization. She'd been trying to reach Jade the wrong way.

All that squinting and straining with her thoughts had been completely useless. Maybe that was how they did it in the movies to look dramatic, but that wasn't the way to reach out with her thoughts. She knew better, because she'd done it in Keyhole Canyon. It wasn't about making an effort, it was about letting go, letting it happen.

Excitement quickened her heartbeat, but she tried to keep her breathing steady and relaxed. She took the time to finish bandaging her thumb, deliberately ignoring the impulse to hurry. She needed to be calm, like when she was working with a nervous horse. Except now it wasn't a skittish horse that she needed to tame— it was her own skittish mind.

Mrs. Jersey and her drum weren't here to help her this time, but she did have the waterfall. Rose focused on the sound of the water tumbling over the rocks and plunging into the pool below, letting her thoughts sink into the rush. She let her mind empty itself into the sound, allowing herself to drift toward the dreamlike state she'd entered back in the desert when she'd forged her mental connection to Jade. She needed that connection now, but if she reached for it, it would slip out of her grasp like smoke. Even the dull throbs of pain from her wounded thumb began to seem like the beats of a drum.

Rose closed her eyes, listened to the rush of the waterfall, and sunk into a trance.

Chapter Eighteen
Triumph Triumphant

Rex Triumph tucked his wings into a dive and shot past Jade. He twisted gracefully in the air and swooped, looping the smaller green dragon in a dazzling show of midair prowess. She nipped at him playfully, catching only air in her teeth. His throat quivered with a warbling trill of delight, and he reveled in the sound of his own true voice again.

He played a harmless game of tag with her as they soared high over the city, but Triumph wanted to show that he was the better flier. Six-winged dragons were born of the air. Compared to Triumph's aerial prowess, an Archon's flying was merely adequate. He danced with the flows of air, shaping the wind with his magic, persuading the capricious gusts to propel him where he wished to go. Next to that, Jade could do little more than clumsily pummel the air with her wings.

He wanted her to be awed by his skills. He needed every edge he could get.

Influencing humans was easy for him. Most were as pliant as the volunteers in a stage hypnotist's show. But dominating another dragon was not as easy. He could sense Jade still had doubts about using the Harbinger to awaken other dragons, so he had to carefully and subtly nudge her desires to serve his ends. Fortunately, she lacked his experience at psychic dueling. She would hardly have been a challenge if not for the human girl.

He had intended to put Rose Gallagher to sleep along with the others. Somehow, Jade had protected the girl. It was clear that the young Archon had formed a real friendship with this child. Such an unnatural idea had never even occurred to Rex Triumph. But Jade was still at the age when hatchlings felt tender and protective toward their nest mates. No doubt she simply viewed this human girl as a surrogate for her siblings.

He had hoped that by separating Jade from Rose, the Archon would shed her doubts. But she still questioned her task.

What will become of the humans? she called out to him over the howling of the wind.

He let out a snort. *They can take care of themselves.*

But we'll be taking their world away from them! Her

green eyes flashed, and he felt the force of her defiance.

Triumph reined in his irritation. As he saw it, only by a stroke of ill luck had humanity's ancestors ever gotten the chance to crawl out from their dirt warrens in the first place. The world was theirs on loan, and dragons deserved to take back their rightful place. Jade was too softhearted to accept that, so he tried a different approach.

They need us, he told her, his voice soothing and wise. *They are lost and miserable.*

Triumph sang a lament for the sad condition of the human race. Had she looked at their faces? Their bodies? They took poisons into their mouths, their lungs, even directly into their blood, never minding the cost on their frail bodies. They squandered their hard-earned money at the gambling table in the pursuit of a momentary illusion of happiness and wasted their short lives trying to escape into the television screen. Could there be a more pitiful creature than the average human in their modern age?

Jade let out a long, mournful cry.

Yet still she balked, the stubborn thing. The green dragon keened at him, calling forth in his mind images of her human companions. *They're not the sad creatures you make them out to be*, she said. She sang of

Rose Gallagher, Clay Ostrom, and Doris Jersey, and he could hear how much affection and respect she had for these humans.

Yet they long for magic, he cooed, looking out over the dazzling lights of Las Vegas. Why else would they make a place such as this and flock here by the millions, even though most come away poorer for it? The glitter, the lights, the thrill, and the wonder—they would pay anything for a taste of enchantment in their dreary existence. *Can you not see how happy you have made your friends by coming into their lives?* Triumph asked, infusing his words with subtle magic. *They turn to you as flowers turn to the sun. If we dragons return, the whole of the human race will have the chance to bask in our glory! Would you deny them?*

Triumph swooped in to look her in the eyes. He could feel her psychic resistance slowly eroding under his pressure.

Dragons will change the world. It will be hard on the humans, she said.

At first, he agreed. *But we will guide them to wisdom and happiness.*

Triumph did believe this, after a fashion. He knew humans needed to know their role in life to feel secure. They would be happier when dragons ruled them and they learned to accept their place in the greater scheme of things.

We must be gentle with them, Jade said. *They will be afraid.*

Yes. His heart soared. He had her.

Triumph guided the young Archon back toward Lost World. He thought about how he had spent so much effort on this place, crafting it so it reminded him of his home and his time. Now he would have so much more than robotic dinosaurs and artificial forests. Jade would use the Harbinger, and they would set the world right again.

He dived toward the roof where his outdoor pool glowed azure next to his penthouse apartment and executed a flawless landing on the high-dive platform. Jade skidded to a halt on the rough concrete, her wings toppling a few of the wrought-iron chairs leaning against the wall. Triumph was settling himself into a composed posture, twitching with eagerness for the Awakening to begin, when he noticed something odd.

A thick red drop oozed from Jade's claw.

From between the fine scales on the claw that held the Harbinger, he saw a trickle of blood seeping forth. A droplet splashed onto the cement. He trilled to her curiously. *Are you injured?*

Jade set down the Harbinger and stared at her

bleeding thumb. *No,* she rumbled. *It's Rose.*

He drew back in shock, the feathers on his neck ruff spreading. *What?*

We are bound by blood, Jade told him. Her words carried into his mind a short mental image of a canyon somewhere in the desert, two girls standing in a circle in the sand with a thudding drum in the background, the sharp flash of a silver blade.

Triumph thrashed his tail so hard that he nearly unbalanced himself. Jade had done much more than form a friendship with a human, the reckless creature. His mind recoiled at the very thought of this strange blood-pact between human and dragon.

She is trying to call me, Jade said. She dipped a talon into her own blood and examined it with a dazed expression. *She is afraid.*

You should... Triumph began, then stopped.

He had started to say that Jade should ignore the feeble human girl-child, but suddenly he realized that an opportunity lay within his grasp.

You should go to her, he crooned.

Jade looked up, blinking her great eyes.

He made his thoughts soothing. *She fears what you intend to do, but she should not. Why not go to her and explain?*

The Archon dipped her head, a posture of uncertainty.

Why do you hesitate? he asked. He brought to bear all his psychic leverage, making his words like a magnet to draw her attention away from the tektite she had so carelessly set aside. *Surely if Rose Gallagher is your friend, she will accept your decision.*

I'm sure she'll come around, Jade said.

He peered at her, adopting an air of mild incredulity. *Then why do you resist the idea of going to her? Do not tell me you fear her reproach so much!*

Of course not! the young Archon said. She drew herself up, projecting all the self-confidence a young dragon could muster. *Wait here. I will be back.*

As you wish, my lady.

Jade rocked back on her haunches and leaped into the air, spreading her wings to catch a gust that bore her aloft. Triumph watched as she banked away, negotiating the swirling currents until she found her balance. She dropped out of sight over the lip of the building, angling her way back toward the construction site of the Triumphant.

Rex Triumph let out a satisfied chirp and dropped from his high perch. He reached with his long, dexterous claws and plucked the Harbinger from beside the pool. He flicked away the drop of Jade's blood that marred the green-gold surface.

Mine.

He didn't need that fickle hatchling anymore, with her tragically sentimental affection for the human race. Now the Harbinger had a more capable wielder, one who would not hesitate to use it as it should be.

Triumph let out a piercing cry, heralding his resolve to the sky and stars and howling wind. By dawn, the humans would awaken to a different world than this gaudy, hollow shell they had fashioned for themselves.

It would be a world ruled by dragons.

Chapter Nineteen

Rose and Jade

A sharp sound of ringing metal shook Rose from her trance. She looked up and saw a flash of vivid color at the edge of her vision. *Jade,* she realized, her heart racing. The green dragon threaded the gaps between girders to make her way down to the waterfall. Her claw rapped against one of the I-beams, making the steel chime.

"Jade!" Rose cried out, standing and waving her hands. She'd done it! She'd managed to reach her friend in time! "Hey, I'm down here—"

I see you.

Dragon language carried much more emotion than words, and the irritation in Jade's voice hit Rose like a shove. Her stomach tightened into a fearful knot, but she drew herself up and faced her friend with her head held high.

"We need to talk!" Rose shouted over the wind.

Jade descended in a tight spiral, then tucked in her wings and dropped the remaining few yards to land with a quivering impact. She arranged herself in a composed, austere posture to face Rose. Only a catlike twitching at the end of her tail betrayed any inner anxiety. *I've made my decision,* she said.

Rose wished Jade would turn back into a human. Translating dragon speech in her head took effort, and Jade's attitude made it harder. "Have you thought about what will happen?" Rose asked. "You might cause a war between dragons and humans. Do you want that?"

Of course not, Jade said. *The return of dragons will be a shock, but humans will adapt.*

Rose heard Rex Triumph's sly words lurking underneath that statement. "It'll be more than a shock. People will be terrified. When we're afraid, we fight."

Many people will welcome us. One of Jade's claws flinched, and she scraped fitfully at the dirt. *Dragons have wisdom to share.*

"What good will that do if people are too scared to listen?"

They will be afraid only at first.

"At first? How long does 'at first' last, huh? Months? Years? How many people and dragons will die 'at first'? You can't know!"

Why do humans have to be so foolish? Jade snarled.

Rose caught echoes of Jade's conversation with Rex Triumph as her mind deciphered the dragon speech. He'd shared a pretty dim view of humanity with Jade. It hardly surprised her, given his condescending attitude back at Lost World, but it did make her mad. What gave Triumph the right to judge humanity? "Oh, like all dragons are perfectly reasonable. I'm sure *no* dragon *ever* loses his temper. I'm sure dragons *never* flip out when things don't go their way or pick a fight when they're mad about something..."

What do you want from me? Jade keened. Her tail uncoiled and thrashed, sending stones and spray flying from the waterfall pool. *I was given the Harbinger! I was given the responsibility to save my people!*

Rose began to respond, but a sudden realization stopped her. "Where is it?"

Jade froze, her tail raised mid-swipe.

"Where's the tektite, Jade?" Rose asked. Her chest clenched.

I...left it. Jade's voice emerged in a low wail. *I left it with Rex Triumph.*

Then Jade let out a shriek that rattled the naked beams of the half-built Triumphant. It hit Rose as a blast of feeling too strong to translate into words—a mixture of rage, fear, and shame that wrenched her heart. She stumbled toward her friend, dizzy as her brain tried to interpret the ululating cry.

"Stop...Jade, please! It's too hard for me to—"

Rose staggered and thumped into the solid, warm wall of Jade's armored flank.

Through that touch, a current of understanding passed between them. They were a different species, born millions of years apart, and yet they had entered a union that bridged the vast gulf between dragon and human. They had shared their blood and thoughts. Their lives were joined. Rose hadn't understood how much she had committed to Jade, how they had chosen to share a common destiny. The revelation hit her in a rush, and she felt her eyes sting with her own shame.

"I'm sorry," Rose said. "I'm so sorry."

The world shimmered, and Jade transformed into her human body.

Rose threw her arms around her friend. "I didn't even think about what you were going through," she said. "All I did was try to stop you from helping your people. I was scared of what would happen."

"I should've listened," Jade whispered. "You were right. Waking up all the dragons at once would be a disaster. But what else am I supposed to do?"

"We'll think of something," Rose said. "We'll think of a way we can bring the dragons back without starting a war. Maybe we'll have to do it a little at a time."

"To get people used to the idea," Jade said. "Yes."

Rose pulled out of the embrace and looked into Jade's eyes, still holding her friend's hands. "But we need to get the Harbinger back. If it's not too—" She bit her lip. "It'll defend itself, and Triumph won't be able to use it, right?"

Jade brushed her hair out of her face. "Well...maybe."

That didn't sound reassuring. "What do you mean?"

"Triumph is strong," Jade said. Rose could feel her friend's hands tremble. "The Harbinger will resist him, but I don't know how long. I don't know its limits or all its secrets."

Rose took a deep breath. "Well then, we have to get it back."

"Yes," Jade said, but her voice quavered. "Rose...I'm afraid of what I'll do."

Rose tightened her grip on Jade's hand. "What do you mean?"

The dragon-girl averted her eyes, and Rose could hear the shame in her voice. "Triumph is clever. Cleverer than me. He tricked me into leaving you behind. He tricked me into letting him steal the Harbinger."

"How?" Rose asked.

"He slipped into my mind and made me careless." Jade shuddered. "I didn't sense him doing it until I got back to you."

"You're on your guard now," Rose said.

"It's not enough!" Jade sounded like she was crying. Rose hadn't ever seen her shed tears. "He's old and cunning, and I don't know if I can stop him! If he could make me forget the Harbinger, what else could he make me do?"

"Jade..."

"I don't know if I can stand up to him," she sobbed. "He's too much for me."

Rose stood for a moment holding her friend's hand, uncertain of how to reassure her. "Look, the things you mentioned—leaving me behind and stealing the Harbinger—he did that when you were a dragon, right?"

Jade blinked at her. "Yes."

"So maybe it will be harder for him to influence you as a human. I think it throws him off. You stopped him from putting me to sleep when you were human."

Jade thought about this, then nodded. "Yes." She managed a fragile smile. "My heart feels different when I'm like this. I don't think he'll be able to trick me as easily."

"Right. We'll try it," Rose said. It wasn't a foolproof plan, but they had to try something. "You stay a human. And you promise not to do anything with the Harbinger unless we both agree. Okay?"

"Okay."

"Let's go, then!" she said, setting off toward the entrance.

The locked gate that had trapped Rose no longer posed a problem. Jade touched the padlock and exerted a bit of magic that made the air shimmer, and the steel loop split.

Rose ran alongside her friend, trying not to let her own fear show. Jade was shaken, and Rose needed to be strong for both of them. But she had no idea what they would do when they reached Rex Triumph. Two human girls against a full-grown dragon? They'd only last as long as it took him to stop laughing.

If Rose couldn't help Jade get her confidence back, they were both done for.

Chapter Twenty

Prehistoric Casino

Rex Triumph set the Harbinger down, his chest heaving with exertion. He had expected the stone to resist him, but the enormity of its power left him awed. Pitting his will against it was like trying to claw down a mountain.

Yet he still believed he could master it, given time. The Harbinger was made to be used. He knew it wanted to be used.

Clearly he could not make the Harbinger awaken other dragons yet. But perhaps it would not be so resistant to a lesser task. Something similar to its true purpose, but on a smaller scale.

Triumph leaned his long head back and let the fierce desert wind tousle his feathers, gathering his strength for the next effort. The wind, ever his ally, brought a fresh scent to his nostrils—one he recognized immediately. Jade, but in her human form, along with Rose Gallagher. They were coming back.

Jade smelled of fear.

If she was afraid to turn into a dragon again and face him, that was fine. She was little danger to him. In fact, if he could bend the Harbinger ever so slightly to his will, he could arrange a special greeting for them.

Triumph peered into the Harbinger and focused his power.

* * *

The powerful winds that swept through town were on the verge of becoming a full-fledged sandstorm. Rose could barely see the casinos at the south end of the strip, the great spotlight on top of the Luxor reduced to a feeble glimmer. Clouds of sand twisted and billowed, and the wind was still rising.

"Come on!" She took hold of Jade's hand and broke into a run. They could still make it to Lost World before the sandstorm arrived in full force.

At least the storm had driven the tourists inside. Traffic was so thin that Rose and Jade had no trouble darting across streets. As they approached Lost World, they passed a pair of women who babbled incoherently, their eyes wild as they clutched their hats to their heads. One had a bloody smear down the side of her face. Rose guessed she must've gotten nailed by a piece of debris.

A shrill cry cut through the din of the storm. Rose slowed her pace. That sounded like an animal. "Did you hear that?"

Jade shielded her face as she answered. "One of those flying things."

"A dragon?" Rose asked.

"No!" Jade looked puzzled. "Wait, do you have them here? I haven't seen any."

"A bird?"

"I've seen *those*," the dragon-girl said.

"A bat?" But Rose knew no bat ever made a sound like that.

"No," Jade said. "It was one of those animals—with wings."

As they approached the plaza to Lost World, they heard the strange cry again, followed by the frightened screams of tourists.

Jade stepped out ahead and pointed. "There! One of those! You do have them."

Rose lurched to a stop, her eyes wide. "A pterodactyl."

"Right!" Jade sounded pleased. "That's it."

The creature was mostly white with black tips on its wings and patches of deep purple around its eyes. The membranes of its wings were faintly striped, the lighter and darker patches blending whenever it flapped. It clung to the edge of a safety rail with thin, powerful claws, wobbling every time a gust of wind rocked its body and squawking with each lurch. A knot of tourists bolted out the front door of the casino, saw the prehistoric creature flailing around on its perch, and fled in a terrified tangle.

"We don't have them," Rose shouted. "They're from your time!"

She looked up and suddenly realized something was missing over the door. Before, a motorized model of a pterodactyl had hung suspended over the entrance to the casino, turning its head and flapping in mock flight. The model was gone. Or rather, she realized, it had changed. Something had brought it to life.

"It's Triumph," Jade said. She looked up at the great stone archway leading into Lost World. "He's learning to use the Harbinger. I don't think he can get it to wake up dragons yet...so he's trying it with these animals first."

Rose's stomach gave a sick tumble. She'd hoped the Harbinger might compel Triumph to throw it away as it had done with her dad. No such luck. "We need to get in there!" Rose eyed the pterodactyl warily. It was probably not much taller than she was if they stood face to face, but its vast wings made it seem immense.

"Don't worry about it," Jade said. "Those only eat fish. It's just annoyed by the wind." She strode forward, waving her arms at the creature. "Go! Find a better perch!"

The pterodactyl drew itself up and glared like a large, indignant umbrella.

"Go!" Jade took a threatening step forward, as if to charge. "Get out!"

With an outraged squeal, the creature hopped away from Jade and spread its wings. The wind caught it like a living kite and swept it aloft. The pterodactyl flapped laboriously against the treacherous current toward a large palm tree. It landed in a great tumult of leathery wings and demolished fronds, then poked its pointed head out from the tree with a look of imperious displeasure.

Jade turned and offered Rose her hand. "They're big cowards. Come on!"

Rose joined her friend, and they raced toward the entrance of Lost World. She could hear more screams as tourists fled through other exits. If the pterodactyl had come to life out here, they were sure to find more dangers inside.

Rose's grip tightened on Jade's hand as they advanced cautiously through the front doors, then stopped and listened.

Every casino she'd ever visited had been crowded

with people, so the emptiness of Lost World was creepy all by itself. Even more unnerving were the strange sounds that filtered through the jungle. Rumbles and muted animal screeches came from every direction. The air felt thick and smelled of earth and pollen, like the rain forests Rose had visited in Hawaii. Whatever Triumph was doing was affecting all of Lost World.

Rose took off at a sprint through the gaming area toward the restaurant, with Jade close at her heels. They were dashing through lanes of abandoned slot machines when a buzzing from Rose's pocket brought her up short.

"A text from Clay!" she said, checking her phone. A jolt of fear shot through Rose as she realized she'd forgotten about Clay and Mrs. Jersey, who were probably still in the Smithsonian Lounge.

"What's it say?" Jade asked.

Rose read aloud. "He says, 'Where are you? Things are getting weird. Can you meet us in the parking lot?'"

She sighed in relief and collapsed onto one of the slot machine stools. "They're okay. They got out."

Her phone buzzed again, and another text appeared. "He says, 'Saw a real triceratops! Think we spooked it.'"

Suddenly, a great trumpeting bellow shook the empty casino.

Jade clamped her hand on Rose's arm. "Run!"

The floor began to shake, and the great chandelier overhead tinkled as its innumerable crystals trembled.

Rose and Jade had only covered a few yards in their retreat when a hulking form came into view, charging like a runaway locomotive down the promenade. Rose had one good look at the three-horned behemoth before it thundered into the gambling hall.

The triceratops plowed its way through banks of slot machines, slamming heedlessly through the aisles. The massive animal's great bulk shattered everything in its path, demolishing scores of slot machines. The juggernaut rammed through the blackjack tables, tossing its mighty horns as playing cards fluttered like a cloud of butterflies in its wake. The mayhem of the beast's rampage washed over Rose in a tidal wave of noise.

Rose and Jade sprinted away, clearing the short flight of stairs from the gambling room in a single hurdle. They skittered around a corner and ran toward the elevators.

"It's not following," Jade said.

Rose looked back the way they'd come, swallowing huge gulps of air. She could still hear the triceratops venting its fury on the slot machines and gaming tables.

"They get like that," Jade said. "When they lose their temper. Best to stay away from them when they're in that kind of mood."

Rose ran her fingers through her tangled hair. At least Jade knew about dinosaurs and how they behaved. Maybe that would be enough to get them through the casino in one piece. "That private elevator is probably the only way to get to Triumph's penthouse," she said. "We need to get back to the Smithsonian Lounge. There should be maps to help guests find their rooms." She led Jade to the check-in counters. "Here's one."

Lost World was designed to funnel all foot traffic through the gambling area, just like all the casinos Rose had ever visited. Normally this did not put the average visitor at risk of being gored to death by an insane dinosaur. Fortunately, Rose knew Jade's magic could get them access to places that were locked off to tourists.

"There's a service corridor that leads through to the promenade," Rose said, pointing to the map. "It's a longer way around, but it'll get us past the triceratops. Come on."

They found the door with the "Employees Only" sign, and Rose asked Jade to open it.

Jade attempted to turn the knob, but it held fast. "It's locked."

"Yeah, I know. Pop it open with magic like you did back at the construction site."

"But this lock is different," Jade said, peering at it uncertainly.

Rose grabbed her friend's hand and placed it on the door. "Just make the metal split. That's easy, right?"

A little shimmer flowed through the air, and the door made a heavy clunking noise. The steel knob dropped off in several chunks, along with the catch and all the locking mechanisms. Freed from its restraints, the door tilted slowly open.

Jade gave it a startled look. "Oh!"

"Let's go!"

They followed a short corridor to the promenade. Rose and Jade ran past empty shops and overturned displays, threading their way back toward the Smithsonian Lounge.

Rose jerked to a stop when she heard something rustle behind them. She whirled and thought she saw a brief flash of movement from a leather goods store.

She picked up her pace.

Another dozen yards or so down the promenade, she heard another noise. This time it was like a sharp chirp, followed by skittering along the tiles. Rose spun and searched for the source of the sound. They rounded a corner to find a large fountain in the middle of a wide circular plaza. Something perched on the concrete rim, drinking the water.

"Velociraptor!" Rose cried.

The dinosaur looked up at her with brilliant golden eyes.

"Oh," said Jade with a sigh of relief. "Just one of those."

Rose gave her a hopeful look. "So they're safe?" In books, movies, and video games about dinosaurs, velociraptors showed up as particularly savage creatures.

"They mostly go after sick or wounded prey." Jade said. "Or eggs."

A trilling call rang out behind them. Two more velociraptors trotted into view, each as big as a wolf and moving with an eerie weightless grace.

"Are you sure?" Rose asked.

Jade furrowed her brow. Another raptor emerged from behind the fountain. Rose saw the reflected light from a pair of eyes within a clothing store, bobbing gently up and down.

"This isn't right," Jade said. "They don't act like this." She flashed a worried look to Rose. "I think Triumph is controlling them."

Rose's heart hammered in her chest. "Why aren't they attacking?"

Jade looked from raptor to raptor. "Maybe he's not in full control," she said. "He's only making them think we're weak."

"Okay...then we have to bluff," Rose said. She knew what to do if she met a bobcat or coyote in the desert. Be confident and don't present them with an obvious target. She also knew it helped to do something confusing or something to make herself look bigger.

"I'm gonna hold them off," she whispered. She swept her gaze over the hunters, making eye contact one by one. Wild cats found eye contact to be intimidating. She hoped it would be the same with velociraptors. "Do you see any closed doors?"

"Yeah," Jade said.

That was good. If the door to a shop or restaurant was closed, it meant no velociraptors would be inside. "Guide us there," she told Jade as she unslung her backpack. "Nice and slow."

She felt Jade's hand on her belt, leading her along. The birdlike predators circled, weaving and bobbing in silent communication with one another as they studied the two girls. The pack gradually edged closer as the girls slowly retreated.

Rose took the folded parka from her backpack and shook it out.

The foremost velociraptor hopped back a few steps and made a clucking noise.

Rose waved the parka in one hand, fishing in her pack with the other. Her fingers found the whistle she carried in case she ever became lost in the desert and needed to call for help. She pressed the whistle to her mouth and blew hard.

The piercing trill echoed through the promenade. Several raptors squeaked in alarm.

It was working! Rose flapped the parka side to side, then over her head, making it as big and intimidating as she could, all while blasting on the whistle. Jade guided her steps in retreat as the hunters circled, sniffing the air and making clicking noises but keeping their distance.

She heard a tap behind her, then the heavy clunk of a push bar on a door. Rose whirled and rushed behind Jade through the open door, slamming it behind them. She leaned against its thick glass surface, trembling with relief.

Then she looked up and recognized where they were.

"This is the Cretaceous Garden," she whispered. Her throat clenched and suddenly she felt like she couldn't breathe. "Oh no..."

Rose had visited the Cretaceous Garden before. It was a sprawling indoor park filled with kid-friendly rides, games, and tourist attractions, all set within a lush prehistoric landscape. It was also the section of Lost World that had the most mechanical dinosaurs. There was a track where tourists could ride on a robot ankylosaurus, a lake with paddle-boats and long-necked elasmosaurus replicas, a fake petting zoo with baby dinosaurs, a carousel full of extinct mounts—and at the center of the Cretaceous Garden, the main attraction stood in all its glory.

A massive head rose over the palm trees, silhouetted against the glow from the tinted glass dome that encased the garden. Rose let out a terrified squeak and clutched Jade's arm.

The Tyrannosaurus rex turned and looked directly at them.

Chapter Twenty-One

Shaping

More than forty feet long, the titanic predator shoved through the palm trees, bringing its entire body into view. Rose gaped in horror at the beast's daggerlike teeth and the eyes that stared straight at her, luminous with reflected light. Rose saw an intelligent gleam in the dinosaur's eyes, almost like recognition—and she felt a terrible intuition that Rex Triumph was firmly in control of this creature. She wouldn't be able to scare it off with a whistle and a flapping parka.

The dinosaur took another step forward, and a shriek tore from Rose's throat.

The air shimmered, and suddenly Jade was there in her true form. She reared up, spreading her wings as far as they could reach, and bared her teeth in a snarl. Rose clutched Jade's hind leg, bracing herself against the armored scales.

The Tyrannosaurus balked at the unexpected appearance of a creature as massive as itself. It pulled itself into a crouch, a ruff of neck spines spreading in an aggressive display, and loosed an ear-shattering bellow. If fifty lions roared in unison, Rose thought it would sound like the challenge issued by the Tyrannosaurus rex.

The response from Jade made the dinosaur's roar sound like a wet sneeze.

Rose screamed along with her friend, yet she could hear nothing of her own voice above the unearthly cry. The resonance transcended mere sound, delivering a powerful psychic challenge to any enemy who dared oppose the dragon. The palm trees trembled and shed their fronds, the gravel danced like popcorn across the ground, and sharp cracks lanced through the glass panels of the Cretaceous Garden's dome.

Jade finished by loosing a jet of bright flame over the head of the Tyrannosaurus.

The dinosaur let out a surprisingly piteous yelp, then spun and lurched away, disappearing into the undergrowth with a crash of cracking timber.

Rose's ears continued to ring from Jade's roar. Even her bones felt like they still hummed. She looked up at her friend, eyes wide with wonder.

The green dragon shimmered, and Jade was a girl again.

"That was incredible!" Rose gasped in a hoarse voice.

"I could feel Triumph in that animal's mind, controlling it to attack us," Jade said. Then she grinned. "I kicked him out."

Rose peered into her friend's emerald eyes. "You beat him!"

Jade ran her fingers through her pale bangs. "Yes. I did. I think it was because of you."

"Me?"

"Being in contact with you helps. I kept a grip on my human side, even as a dragon."

Hearing that startled Rose. It was one thing that Jade could change her body to look like a human being, but now it sounded like she was even thinking of herself as partly human. It was no longer just a disguise, but an element of her identity. If Jade felt confident about changing back to a dragon, that would save them a whole lot of trouble.

"We don't need the elevator," Rose said. "You can fly us to the penthouse."

Jade nodded. "Right!" But after a second, she looked less certain. "Maybe I could carry you in my claws this time."

Rose thought Jade looked faintly embarrassed. Was this some issue of dragon dignity? Perhaps she felt ashamed to have Rex Triumph see her being ridden by a human. Rose thought about Jade's talons, and what might happen if she made one wrong twitch while they were flying. "I don't know if that'll be safe."

Jade fiddled with her hair. "It's just that it's windy and we don't have any rope or cables this time, and I'm afraid if I mess up, you'll fall off."

"Oh!" That was a good point, but a solution occurred to Rose. "I've got an idea."

The ankylosaurus ride in the Cretaceous Garden was mostly for little kids, letting them ride a plodding robot dinosaur around a sandy track. What Rose cared about was the big saddle the thing wore over its armored hide. She was pretty sure she could rig the saddle girth into a good strap for her to hold on to Jade in flight. She just didn't know how to get it off a living ankylosaurus.

When they jogged into view of the ride, they saw the tank-like dinosaur gnawing away at a clump of ferns. The discarded remains of the creature's saddle lay in the sand—the leather had split when the dinosaur suddenly expanded upon coming to life. Fortunately, this dinosaur showed no signs of being compelled to attack them. Triumph seemed to have given up on that tactic.

Rose examined the saddle. "The latigo's broken," she said, fingering the thick strap that held the girth strap in place. "You think you can magic it back together?"

"Maybe," Jade said, cocking her head to examine it. "But I don't know if I can shape it right to make it fit."

Rose had only been thinking of making a neck strap to hold, but if Jade could magically remake the saddle to conform to her own body, that would be a lot more secure. Especially when they confronted Rex Triumph. Jade might need to do more than just navigate through tricky winds.

"That would be great!" Rose said. "Way better than jumper cables. So what's the problem?"

"I don't know how. It's not the sort of thing dragons do." Jade bit her lip and took a few uncertain steps, circling the broken saddle. "I don't see what to make it become."

"Can I help?" Rose asked.

Jade's expression brightened. "Yes! Just like you did back at the door."

"The door? What did I do?"

"You showed me what you wanted when we broke the lock on that door. I could see it when you took my hand. I saw how the door worked and everything, and where to make the metal fracture." She looked at the saddle, then back at Rose. "This is more complicated, but I think we can do it."

"Okay," Rose said. "Are you going to turn into a dragon?"

Jade shook her head. "It's easier when we're both human to...um..."

"Get in tune?"

"Yes." Jade stood there and looked expectantly at Rose.

Rose took a deep breath, then knelt in the sand and placed their hands on the saddle. When she closed her eyes, her imagination conjured up an image of Jade as a dragon that was startling in its clarity. Rose guessed that Jade was helping somehow. "The seat's much bigger than it has to be." The saddle was meant to hold several tourists at once. "Let's start by reshaping the saddle-tree." This was the part that gave the saddle its shape.

She opened her eyes to check their progress, but the world seemed to go swimmy and she squeezed her eyelids shut again. "I want two girth straps," she said. "One that goes in front of the wing joint and one behind, anchored at the cantle."

The dragon saddle took shape in her mind, flowing into a new configuration as Rose spoke. She drew on her knowledge of tack accumulated from a lifetime of dealing with horses. She felt the leather surface distend under her hands, its very substance becoming like liquid to be shaped by Rose's artistic imagination and the power of Jade's magic.

"Jumping stirrups," she whispered, and heard the creak of warping metal.

Her breath came in shallow drafts now. Maintaining this kind of concentration took as much effort as scaling a steep mountain face. She checked over the image of her handiwork in her mind. "Safety straps," she rasped. "Quick-release carabineers."

That was all she could think of. Rose opened her eyes.

The saddle was exactly as she had envisioned—and then some. To her surprise, exquisitely tooled patterns adorned the leather, carved into images of twining dragons all around the edges of the saddle. What had once been dull brown leather now glistened as if it had just been oiled, beautiful enough to take into the show ring. It was the kind of tack she'd always longed to own but could never afford.

"It's wonderful," she whispered.

"Yes," Jade said, staring at Rose with wide eyes. "That was different from any shaping I've ever done. Human language is amazing."

"It is?" Rose had assumed Jade found plain, old English to be inadequate. Dragon speech seemed to carry so much more information, conveying emotions and experiences directly into another person's head.

"You put names to everything," Jade said. "Those names hold the world in place."

Rose scratched her head. "Our language doesn't do anything special."

"Yes it does. Just like your minds."

"Hmm." Rose scratched her head. "I never thought of language that way." She turned her attention to the saddle. "Let's get this on you."

Jade shifted back into her dragon form, and to Rose's delight, the saddle was a perfect fit. After adjusting the straps and making sure all lay well, Rose settled into place on Jade's back. "Does it feel good?"

Yes.

"All right then, let's—" Rose suddenly realized they were still inside the hotel. Jade would have to turn human again to fit through the doors. "Oh, darn it! We'll have to take this off and put it back on again once we get outdoors."

No we won't, Jade growled and unleashed a streak of flame toward the roof.

This blast dwarfed the warning shot she'd used to

frighten the Tyrannosaurus. The brilliant bolt she spat forth at the ceiling flew like a small meteor. A gaping hole exploded in the translucent roof of the Cretaceous Garden. Rose yelped in surprise and covered her head with her hands against glass shrapnel, but Jade simply folded her wings, shielding them both from the debris. Neither the falling shards nor the molten blobs of glass left a mark on her.

Outside, the sandstorm lashed the Las Vegas sky, howling its fury. "Let's go see Rex Triumph," Rose called. "He's got something that belongs to you."

Chapter Twenty-Two

Duel

Rex Triumph saw the fireball rip into the sky.

He clutched the Harbinger tight in his claw. Despite the stone's reluctance, he'd made it work for him. He'd brought long-lost creatures back to life. Soon he would figure out how to do the same with dragons. Then he would reshape the world to his desires. When he mastered the Harbinger, he could choose to bring back only the dragons that would recognize him as their ruler. He could control the younger and more pliable ones. The elders who might try to take his territory would remain asleep.

The Harbinger was the key to his future. He refused to give it up.

Triumph peered over the side of the hotel and saw the green dragon with the human girl on her back rising through what was left of the roof of the Cretaceous Garden.

He drew back, his neck feathers bristling with astonishment. It was one thing to harbor a tender spot for her human pet, but to go so far as to let the child ride her like some beast of burden...He snorted in disdain. She was unworthy of the Harbinger.

But could he defeat her?

She'd thrown off his domination once already, and he did not relish the notion of a physical duel with an Archon. In battle, they were fearsome to behold. Jade's near-impervious scales could repel all but his most perfect strikes, and he had no comparable weapon to her fiery breath at his disposal. He could outfly her, but that would not save him forever.

Triumph looked at the rising figure of his enemy. His gaze focused on the tiny human girl on Jade's back. That was her weakness.

Triumph settled into position on the roof, cool and poised. He knew what to do.

* * *

Rose leaned forward as far as her safety straps would allow, holding tight to Jade's neck spines and shielding her eyes against the sandstorm. As they took on altitude, they climbed above the worst of the storm's fury and the sand thinned out.

She saw Rex Triumph the moment they crested the

roof, sitting unperturbed by the illuminated waters of his penthouse's swimming pool. Even with all his ornate feathers, the furious wind seemed to do no more than caress him, causing his fantastic plumage to sway in undulating waves across his sinewy body. As much as Triumph terrified her, Rose could not deny his beauty. He seemed somehow more alive than the world around him, even more brilliant than the neon decorations of Las Vegas.

He held the Harbinger in one claw.

Jade skimmed the roof and dropped down on the opposite side of the pool, her talons scraping gouges in the cement as she ground to a halt. Triumph watched with an air of regal indifference. His golden eyes locked with Jade's emerald ones.

Give me back my stone, Jade trilled.

Rose felt none of the disorientation she usually did when her mind tried to comprehend dragon speech. Maybe she was getting better at translating, but she suspected her growing bond with Jade had more to do with it.

Rex Triumph examined the green-and-gold tektite. *It is mine now.*

It was never yours, Jade countered.

"You stole it!" Rose said.

Silence, the six-winged dragon commanded.

Rose felt a brief clenching of her throat, but it vanished instantly. Triumph could not compel her into silence now. "Dream on, loser!" she shouted.

You can't use the Harbinger, Jade said. *It's beyond you. I have been using it.*

"Ha!" Rose said. "All you've done is bring your stupid dinosaurs to life."

Triumph sniffed, unruffled. *Mastery will come with practice.*

Jade clicked her tongue. *No. You only care about yourself. You want the Harbinger for your own power, not for the benefit of dragonkind. It will never be yours.*

It's mine now. And I shall keep it, Triumph rumbled.

Smoke billowed up from Jade's jaws. *Then we have a problem.*

Rose's hands clenched on Jade's spines. She wondered if Jade would hit Triumph with one of her giant fireballs and blow him straight back to the Cretaceous Era.

Shall we have a game? Triumph said.

Rose suddenly remembered what Jade had told her in the Excalibur about the games of dragons. If two dragons could agree on rules, they would stick to them. Triumph was offering a contest to decide who would possess the Harbinger, and if Jade agreed, she would have to abide by the result. "Be careful," Rose whispered to her friend. "It might be a trick."

What sort of game? Jade asked.

The six-winged dragon examined the Harbinger. *A simple one,* he said. *If you can make me let it go, then it is yours. If you cry off the chase, the Harbinger is mine.*

Rose furrowed her brow. "What's the catch?"

I accept, Jade trumpeted.

"Wait!" Rose cried, but the dragons were already moving.

Triumph catapulted himself into the air, unfurling his wings to catch a gust that bore him over the edge of Lost World. Jade barely cleared the ground before he was out of sight.

"Why didn't you wait?" Rose shouted over the wind.

The game is to make him let it go, Jade said. *If I can get one good hit in, he'll probably drop the Harbinger.*

Rose felt the dragon's body change underneath her. Her scales expanded, each one growing thicker and broader, overlapping to provide more reinforcement. The muscles in her chest swelled, lending greater power to her wings. Her talons lengthened and honed themselves to fine points.

Triumph is overconfident, Jade said. *He will try to use his psychic influence to make me give up. It won't work.*

"Why not?"

Because I have you with me, she said. *Together, I know we can—*

Jade let out a peal of surprise and wheeled in the air. A mass of iridescent color tore through the space they had just occupied, jostling them with a smack of a feathery tail as it passed. Rose saw Triumph pull out of his power dive and dart away.

He's...really fast, Jade said, not sounding quite as confident.

"Where is he?" Rose asked, her heart thundering as she searched the skies.

Triumph appeared again, arcing over the top of Lost World before plummeting toward them with his killer claws outstretched.

This time, Jade spat a burst of flame to meet him. The wind caught the streak of fire and twisted it like ribbons. Triumph swooped out of the line of fire, skimming over the face of the hotel. Jade turned her head to track him with her flames. Windows exploded as the flaming lance touched them, and Rose heard screams from within the rooms.

"Stop!" she shouted. "There are people inside!"

The green dragon bit off her fiery attack, and Triumph darted out of sight once more.

"He keeps popping out of nowhere!" Rose said. "Get farther from the buildings!"

Jade changed direction and headed away from Lost World, soaring over the Strip. Rose scanned in every direction, searching for their enemy through sand-blurred vision. She recognized the outlines of the casinos she knew—the Mirage, Caesars Palace, the Luxor—but caught no sight of Rex Triumph.

"Double back. Stay where the lights are brightest." Rose said. She would've preferred to take the fight away from the city, but in the dark with all this sand, they wouldn't have a prayer of spotting Triumph.

Jade leaned against the wind to brake with her wings, and at that instant, Triumph erupted from underneath them, raking Jade's flanks with his scythe-like claws. He'd been flying in a blind spot, close to Jade's rear and just below Rose's line of sight. For a chaotic moment, everything became a blur of flapping wings and rushing feathers. Then Triumph broke off again, streaking away from them with the wind at his back.

Flames gathered in Jade's jaws, but she choked back her attack and belched a spray of embers. Triumph had positioned himself in front of another hotel.

"No!" Rose screamed. "He's using human shields!"

He won't...get away!

There was strain in Jade's voice now. Rose looked over her friend's body. She could see a splash of scarlet against Jade's green scales along her side near her rear leg. "You're hurt!"

It's nothing.

Jade strained to keep pace as Triumph fled, always keeping himself positioned in front of buildings so she couldn't risk using her fiery breath. Jade swooped and soared, searching for an angle of attack that wouldn't endanger innocent lives.

Rose leaned flat against her friend, willing Jade to go faster, searching for the opportunity to strike.

It came as Triumph veered toward the empty construction zone of the Triumphant. There was nobody Jade could hurt in the deserted site. "Hit him now!"

Jade responded instantly. A comet-like blast of fire erupted from her jaws and streaked toward her enemy. The other dragon wheeled to escape the attack. On a calm day, she would likely have hit him, but a burst of wind lifted Triumph just out of the line of fire. Steel exploded where Jade's attack struck bare girders, and a portion of the partially built structure crumpled and caved in. The avalanche of metal filled Rose's head with agonizing noise, driving into her ears like spikes.

Triumph pirouetted with a dancer's grace and rode

the wind directly into their flight path. His brilliant feathers filled Rose's vision, and suddenly she saw his killer claw raised over her, poised to split her in half. She shrieked and threw up her hands in a hopeless defensive gesture.

Wrenching herself in the air, Jade managed to get her wing in the path of Triumph's attack just before the deadly claw struck. Rose could hear a terrible meaty sound as the claw bit into the flesh just above Jade's wing joint.

With a piercing howl of pain, Jade twisted in the air, so she was upside down with her whole body between Triumph and Rose. The world spun crazily around Rose's head as she held on with all her might. Jade opened her jaws and unleashed a torrent of furious energy. This was no fiery streak or a meteor-like missile. It was a pillar of raw power, burning white like magnesium, lighting up the sky like a dozen suns. If it had struck Rex Triumph, it would've reduced him to ash.

But it came nowhere close. The six-winged dragon kicked off Jade's chest and looped away, easily evading the attack.

Jade plummeted from the sky. She contorted her body in the air to try to right herself, tail lashing for balance. She struck a girder and bounced off, then managed with tremendous effort to level herself out roughly parallel to the ground. Her claws touched down for a moment on the sidewalk, just enough to kick back up into shaky flight. All the writhing movements tossed Rose violently in her saddle. She felt like a punching bag pummeled by a heavyweight boxer.

Jade struggled for altitude.

Triumph hovered over them.

That is twice I could have killed the human, the six-winged dragon warbled.

In the distance, Rose heard sirens blaring. She coughed violently, trying to get a clean breath of air into her lungs. Her skin felt hot where she had been exposed to the radiance of Jade's last attack.

Do you cry off the chase, little hatchling? Triumph taunted.

No! Jade said.

He puffed up his feathers like a preening bird. *You cannot defeat me,* he sang. *I will give you the chance to think about what is more important to you: the Harbinger, or your friend's life. Find me at Lost World when you are ready to concede.*

With that, he struck off into the storm and was out of sight.

Rose watched him go, her body aching in a hundred

places. He was so fast and so confident that none of Jade's strikes had even come close to him.

How were they supposed to beat him?

Chapter Twenty-Three

Diamond Gambit

Rose's whole body throbbed with each of Jade's shuddering wingbeats as the dragon descended into the construction site and landed with a heavy thud.

Thirsty, moaned Jade. She had brought them back to the waterfall that had once contained the sleeping Rex Triumph. Jade limped over to the pool and plunged her face into the water. Steam rose from her jaws, which still glowed with heat in the aftermath of her attacks. Her throat pulsed as she took ravenous gulps of the cool water.

With fumbling fingers, Rose unclasped herself from her harness and slid to the ground. She staggered over and dunked her head into the water too, rubbing the grit out of her eyes in the soothing water. Her baked skin tingled. When she took a drink, it felt like liquid heaven on her abused throat.

She pulled back from the water and looked over at Jade. The green dragon crouched, her chest heaving with each breath. Rose could see her wounds clearly now. The one on her flank seemed minor, just a shallow gash in the space where her rear leg joined with her body, but the one on her wing joint looked much worse. A stream of blood flowed from the gouge and spattered red drops onto the ground.

Rose spotted a bucket full of tools a little way off. She fetched it and dumped out the contents so she could use the container to wash her friend's wounds.

As she got close, Rose could see the heat shimmer that accompanied Jade's magic rising above the dragon's injuries like baked air off a salt flat. She scooped out some of the water and poured it on, and Jade sighed with relief. The air wavered, and Jade transformed into a human girl again.

She still had a gash on her shoulder and her shirt was ripped, as if Triumph's attack had cut the human clothes along with her dragon body. Now that she thought of it, Rose didn't really understand what happened to Jade's clothing when she changed back and forth. Rose noticed the dragon-girl wore a necklace of braided leather she hadn't seen before. She guessed that was the saddle, changed to fit her friend's new form.

Rose pointed at the wound. "Is that okay?" It was much deeper than the little cut Jade had healed in Keyhole Canyon.

"It'll be fine," Jade replied. As she rubbed her shoulder, a trace of her magic surrounded the gash, and it slowly grew fainter.

Rose gripped Jade's arm and stared intently into her face. "I'm the one he's targeting. You should leave me behind."

"I can't."

"I'm a weak spot! If it wasn't for me, you could fight him."

The dragon-girl shook her head. "I need you." She took Rose's hands and looked into her eyes with such affection that Rose felt like her heart would break. "He could overwhelm my mind if I'm alone. You protect me."

Rose threw her arms around Jade, a painful sob clenching her throat. "I'm sorry!"

"Don't be," Jade whispered, embracing her in return. "We can still win."

Rose didn't see how. As long as Rose rode with Jade, her friend was crippled. Triumph would keep going after Rose, and Jade would have to put herself in his way to save her friend from his deadly claws.

Rose leaned her head against Jade's, holding her tight as she wished for some idea, some spark of inspiration to help them out of this situation.

A sharp pain stung her ear as she pressed it against Jade's scalp. She pulled back, her hand reaching up to touch her mother's diamond earring.

Her gaze drifted over the hard earth of the lot, lingering for a moment on the spot where she had stood hours before, as Jade brought Rex Triumph to life. The memory of black powder swirling through the air rushed back to her. For a moment, time seemed to stop.

"If I'm protecting you," Rose said, "then we need something to protect me."

"I can keep you safe," Jade said, raising her chin.

"I have a better idea!"

Rose led Jade over to where several barrels were piled together. She found what she was looking for in a moment—graphite powder.

"We can use this to protect us!" she told her friend. She grabbed a handful of the fine dust and let it run through her fingers. "Graphite powder is a dry lubricant for a lot of the machines on construction sites," she said. "It works better in the heat. It's basically pure carbon."

"Oh, carbon," Jade said. "Dragons work with that all

the time. It's very versatile." She favored Rose with a puzzled frown. "But it's not going to be much protection. It's soft."

Rose took Jade's hand and pressed her fingers against one of her mother's diamond earrings. "Not always. When carbon's like this, it's the hardest substance in the world."

Through their touch, Rose could feel as Jade's mind dove into the diamond, her perceptions narrowing smaller and smaller like she was flipping through the magnifications of a microscope, until she was sensing the invisible world of atoms and molecules, probing the structure of dense-packed carbon with feelers of psychic energy.

Jade drew back, looking back and forth between the diamond and the black powder. "They are the same! I didn't know you could do that," she said, speaking directly to the graphite like someone praising a pet. "That is very clever!"

Rose visualized the suit of plate mail they had seen at the Excalibur and recalled Clay's comments about modern protective gear. "Dragon Skin armor," she said. "Oh yeah."

Jade's eyes sparkled with excitement. She understood.

"Can we do it?" Rose asked.

Jade touched the earring. "Yes. She wants to protect you."

Rose blinked in surprise, not understanding Jade's words, but the dragon was already getting to work. "Right," Rose said, "we've got to do this right and catch him by surprise." Her gaze came to rest on the pile of tools she had dumped out of the bucket. A heavy bricklayer's trowel rested on the earth. "We need to hit him when he least expects it."

* * *

Rex Triumph flew high above Lost World, reveling in his inevitable victory.

Jade and her human pet had failed. Somehow contact with the girl allowed Jade to resist his psychic coercion, but the cost of such protection was steep. The Archon stood no chance while she had to safeguard her fragile passenger, no matter how much energy she squandered on her flashy attacks. Jade would either leave the girl behind, which would allow Triumph to overcome the other dragon's psychic defenses, or bring the girl with her into battle again and be effectively crippled. Either way, he would overcome.

He hoped Jade would do the wise thing and yield. It would be a waste to have to kill her.

He did not have to wait long. He saw the shadowy

figure of the Archon as she winged her way down the Strip, struggling to hold her course against the winds. As she grew closer, he could make out the passenger she bore on her back. The human had wrapped herself in some kind of parka, a thin cloak that offered her flimsy skin some protection against the sandstorm. It snapped and fluttered around her body like a stunted parody of Jade's majestic wings.

The Archon let out a battle cry as she approached.

Triumph gnashed his teeth in anticipation. Jade and her human pet had chosen to fight. That suited him fine. Now that the Archon was tired out from their earlier battle, he felt confident he could neutralize her in a psychic duel once Rose Gallagher was out of the way. Jade's knowledge might enable him to use the Harbinger more effectively.

Triumph spread his brilliant wings and caught the rushing air currents. He positioned himself above and behind his enemy, where she couldn't bend her neck to target him. She would have to roll over in the air to take aim with her fire breath, effectively destroying her own ability to maneuver. Her attacks would be clumsy and inaccurate, easy to avoid.

He watched Jade struggle to gain more altitude in a vain attempt to achieve a better firing position.

Too slow, he growled. *Much too slow.*

Triumph tucked into a dive and plunged at her from the rear, his claws poised to strike. Jade tried to dodge, but he was too swift, too sure. He lashed his foot out at blinding speed to eviscerate Rose Gallagher.

His claw sheared through her parka, then struck something *hard*.

Triumph saw it only for a split second as the shredded parka whipped away in the wind. The human girl was armored head to toe in brilliant crystal. Scales like a dragon's covered her torso and back, sleeves of gemstone encased her arms and legs, and curved plates like a lobster shell protected her joints. It had all been woven into her clothes, anchored in place by the fabric underneath. Her hood had been turned into a helmet, complete with an impenetrable visor to protect her face and eyes.

She was like a knight in diamond armor.

Triumph's claw cracked where it had struck her.

The momentum of his dive slammed him into the Archon's body, and suddenly he was pressed with his belly against her back, the human girl sandwiched between them. The position left him no room to strike again. He tried to push off and get some distance, but Jade's tail snapped up like a whip to tangle around his own tail, her sharp spines biting deep into his flesh. He couldn't pull away.

Then a sharp, terrible pain exploded in his shoulder joint. Triumph let out a shriek that split the night.

* * *

Rose couldn't see what she was doing. Triumph had landed on top of her, crushing her against Jade's back with his thrashing attempts to escape Jade's grappling tail. But she didn't need to aim. Gripping the handle of the trowel in both hands, she rammed her weapon directly into the feathery mass over her head.

The blade bit deep. They had coated the tool in a solid sheath of diamond, shaping a long, wedge-shaped blade from the carbon. The edge was sharp as broken glass and far harder than steel.

Triumph's scream of pain ripped through the air, a horrible resonance like razors scraping across ten thousand piano strings. Blood splashed down from the wound.

The entangled dragons fell.

Rose could see nothing in the chaos, but her stomach pitched as they plummeted through the air. She felt Jade's muscles pumping as the dragon beat her wings in a desperate effort to control their descent...

They plunged into water.

Blue light shone through the churning waters. The taste of chlorine filled Rose's mouth. She realized they'd landed in Rex Triumph's swimming pool. Her safety straps suddenly snapped as the dragons thrashed in the pool, and she sank like a hammer to the bottom.

Something green glowed next to her hand. *The Harbinger!*

Rose snatched the stone. She tried to rise, but the armor was much too heavy.

Her lungs already burned, and a panicky need for air threatened to overwhelm her. She searched desperately in the turbulent water for a ladder that could lead her out, lead her to air...

Something took hold of her arm and hauled her up.

She broke the surface with a terrific splash and looked up to find herself facing Rex Triumph's teeth locked around the hand that held the Harbinger.

Give me that, he hissed and bit down.

Dragon teeth met diamond armor and cracked. Blood sprayed out of Triumph's mouth as he let out a keen of pain, but he did not let go. He took hold of Rose's body in his foreclaws. She struggled helplessly as he tightened his grip around her armored torso. Triumph pulled with his mouth, trying to wrench her arm out of its socket.

Rose let out a shriek as hot agony shot through her shoulder. The diamond gauntlet slipped in Triumph's blood-slicked jaws, forcing him to struggle for a better grip. Then something bowled him over from behind, and Rose tumbled through the air.

Her body slammed into the concrete and rolled. The armor protected her from the worst of the impact, but it still knocked the air out of her lungs. As her ribs shuddered with racking coughs, she forced her head up to see if there was another attack coming.

Jade clung to Triumph's back, her claws dug into his feathers, her tail wrapped around his hindquarters, and her wings folded over him in full-body grapple. Before he had a chance to use his greater size to throw her off, she plunged her head down and sank her teeth into the base of his neck. Triumph let out a screech.

The feathers and flesh sizzled under Jade's bite. Fire licked up between her teeth.

"I've...I've got it!" Rose spluttered. She managed to lift her arm a few inches off the ground, holding up the Harbinger for them both to see. "He dropped it." Her body convulsed again as she coughed, but she managed to squeak out, "We won."

For a moment, the dragons remained frozen in place. Triumph's legs curled up beneath him, ready to kick out and try to throw his attacker off his back. Jade was poised to unleash a point-blank death strike directly into her enemy's neck.

Then the great six-winged dragon drooped. His feathers flattened against his skin, making him appear to deflate. Rex Triumph bowed his head in defeat.

Chapter Twenty-Four

Change the World

Rose had no idea how much her diamond armor weighed, but at the moment it was much more than her exhausted muscles could bear. She lay spread-eagled by Triumph's pool.

Then the air shimmered, and suddenly Jade knelt over her, her human eyes full of concern.

"Are you all right?" she asked.

Rose managed a little nod. "We didn't make any way to take this stuff off."

They had molded the armor to fit her body, but Rose hadn't thought enough ahead to consider how to remove the crystal mail.

"Don't worry," Jade said. "It remembers the way it was before." The dragon-girl swept her hand over Rose's body. Plates of diamond dissolved into powder, reverting to graphite. The powder puffed up into clouds around Rose and twirled away on the wind.

She held her hand up into the cloud, letting some of the powder stick to her damp skin as the rest blew off into the storm. "Thank you," she whispered, then touched her mother's diamond earring. "Here," Rose said, handing the Harbinger to Jade. "It's yours."

Jade took the stone with solemn dignity. They heard a heavy sigh from the other side of the pool, where Rex Triumph still lay in his ruined splendor.

"We need to talk," Jade said to him. "Become human again to make it easier."

If you wish, the six-winged dragon said.

The air swirled around him like a dust devil, and then Rex Triumph slouched before them in his human form. Misery was written in every line on his face.

Jade took Rose's hand, and they approached him together.

"I didn't lie to you," Jade said. "I will awaken our kind. All of them."

Triumph ran his fingers through his hair. His golden robes were sodden with water, hanging in limp folds from his body. A bloody patch darkened his left shoulder. "When will you get around to this little task, my lady?" he asked.

"It is not little," she said. "It is a sacred trust."

"Then what are you waiting for?"

Jade looked at Rose, then back to their vanquished foe. "Humans must be prepared. That too is a sacred trust. They must be ready to accept us as part of their world."

He scoffed. "They never will."

"We will," Rose said. "You just...have to give us time."

"Time?" He raised a mocking eyebrow. "Speak to me of time when you have waited sixty-five million years." He turned to Jade. "What will you do?"

"I don't know," Jade admitted.

"Humans will not accept the truth. Not unless you shove it in their faces. And then they will react as they always do. With their guns, their armies, their fear."

"Only if we're afraid," Rose said. "We can be better than you think."

He studied her for a moment, then shrugged. "We shall see. You've won this game, so the stone is yours."

"Yes," Jade said.

He winced as if in pain, then looked up at her. "You must do something for me." He paused, taking a deep breath. "The dinosaurs in this building. Turn them back to what they were before."

Despite all he had put Rose and Jade through, the look of utter sorrow on his face made Rose's heart ache. She recognized that the creatures were part of his world, part of everything he missed from the time when his kind had lived. She thought she finally understood why he'd done what he had, at least a little.

Jade also looked sad at the prospect. "Maybe there is some way to leave them."

He shook his head. "No. At least not until you fulfill your promise. Then we shall see. In the world that dragons make, I think there will be room for them again, yes?"

"What about all the video?" Rose asked. "Your security cameras will show how they came to life, and you have to bet some tourists took pictures too."

Triumph waved his hand, dismissing her concern. "Yes, yes. People think so much of these things. It is a two-edged sword, you might say. If they do not see it on the news, then it must never have happened. You see?"

Rose bit her lip. "I don't know."

"Trust me on this matter, Rose Gallagher. I will make these pictures and videos disappear." He grinned at her, a flash of his old cocky demeanor returning. "It will be the easiest thing in the world." He turned back to Jade. "Revert the dinosaurs. Please, Lady Jade."

"Very well," Jade said, and held the Harbinger in both hands.

This time, Rose heard the magic, like a soft chime

from a crystal bell—not really a physical sound, but a single pure note that rang somewhere in her soul. A barely visible pulse spread out from the glowing green-and-gold tektite, rippling down into the resort below, turning the flesh-and-blood dinosaurs back into animated machines. Part of Rose felt the loss almost as keenly as the two dragons. The dinosaurs had been magnificent.

* * *

The paramedics were examining Rose when Mrs. Jersey and Clay shoved their way through the crowd of reporters, police, and tourists. "Rose!" the teacher called. "Rose, my dear, there you are!"

She and Jade were in the open-air parking lot behind Lost World where the rescue workers had set up to care for the distressed tourists and staff. Rose would have liked to simply fly straight home and avoid the crowds and confusion, but she didn't want to leave without Mrs. Jersey and Clay.

"Hi, guys," she said, shrugging off the paramedic who was inspecting her head. "I'm fine," she told him. "You can help someone else."

"You should get to a doctor," the paramedic said, but he left her to her friends.

"There were dinosaurs everywhere!" Clay exclaimed, the words bubbling out in a rapid stream. "What happened? Where's Mr. Triumph? I texted you about a million times, but you never answered."

"My phone broke," Rose said. She'd checked it after she and Jade had gotten down from the roof, but it had not survived the battering she'd put it through. She wondered if her father had been trying to reach her too.

As if summoned by her thoughts, a familiar pickup truck hurtled into the parking lot. It screeched to a halt next to a fire truck, and her father lurched out. "Rose?" he shouted.

"Dad!"

She took off at a run, all her exhaustion disappearing as she rushed to embrace him. He caught her in full stride and lifted her off the ground, enfolding her in his strong arms. His stubble pressed against her damp cheek.

"You're safe," he gasped. His hands checked her head, her arms, and her back as if he could not believe she was really there. "Oh God, you're safe, Rose."

"I'm okay," she said.

If time stopped in that moment and suspended her in the safety of her father's embrace, she would be perfectly happy.

"What on earth happened to you?" he asked, pulling back to get a better look at her.

She knew she looked like a mess. She was bruised

and cut in a dozen places, and a dip in Triumph's pool had not washed off all the sweat, dirt, and ash coating her body. Though the strangest part of her appearance was her clothes. Loops of twisted fabric stuck out from her hoodie and her jeans where they had secured the diamond plates of her armor, making her look like she'd been run through some kind of giant cheese grater. "It's not as bad as it looks," she said.

Her dad looked around at the jam of police cars and emergency vehicles, his rugged face illuminated by swirling blue-and-red light. "I could barely hear you when you called," he said. "But I heard you say *bomb*. I called the Las Vegas cops, and they said there was some kind of crisis...a gas leak or something. People having hallucinations. What happened?"

Mrs. Jersey patted him on the arm. "It's been a very confusing night, Sam," she said.

"Doris?" He seemed to recognize her for the first time. "What's going on?"

"I think the best thing is to get Rose home," Mrs. Jersey said.

"No," Rose interrupted.

Mrs. Jersey blinked at her in surprise.

Rose looked the teacher in the eye. "We need to tell the truth."

She heard Clay draw in a sharp breath beside her.

Mrs. Jersey raised her eyebrows. "I see, dear."

"The truth?" Her father's tone sharpened. "What do you mean? Doris, just what exactly is going on here?"

"Come with me, Dad," Rose said. She thought for a moment that he might balk, but he trailed along after her, followed by her friends.

Rose found a spot blocked out of sight of the rest of the crowd by a cinder-block wall. She held out her hand and beckoned Jade over to her.

"What's this all about?" her father asked.

"It'll be much easier to show you," Rose replied. She turned to Jade. "Okay. Go ahead."

Her father began to say something, but the words died in his throat. Suddenly, he found himself staring up into the eyes of a dragon. His mouth dropped open. He wavered dangerously on his feet, and Rose hurried to his side to hold him up.

His grip tightened on her shoulder. His jaw worked, but no sound came out.

"This is the new friend I've been spending so much time with," Rose said. "I may have forgotten to mention she's a dragon."

Jade bowed her head low and gazed at him with her brilliant-green eyes.

"I know you," he whispered. "I saw you. At the dam. I saw you."

Jade let out a low rumble. She held out her foreclaw, then turned it over to reveal the Harbinger. Rose's father looked at the green-and-gold stone, his eyes wide with astonishment.

"That stone," he croaked. "That...tektite."

The air shimmered, and Jade was a human girl again, wearing an impish smile.

He ran his hand across his brow, rubbing his eyes. "I don't...Was that real?" He stared at Jade. "Am I hallucinating or something? The news reports said..." He trailed off.

Mrs. Jersey stepped up and took Rose's father gently by the arm. "Sam, this is going to take some getting used to. But I promise you, it's not a dream, nor is it a hallucination. Come, let's sit you down for a moment. You look faint." The teacher led him toward a nearby bench, pausing a moment to look back over her shoulder. "Give me a moment with your father, Rose."

As the teacher guided Rose's father away, murmuring soothing words to him, Clay leaned in and spoke in an urgent voice. "What happened with Triumph? Did you find out what the Harbinger is?"

Rose filled Clay in on everything that had happened

since Triumph put him to sleep. By the time she finished telling him about the duel for the Harbinger, his face was slack with awe. "Wow," he said. "Oh wow. I wish I'd been there."

She shuddered at the memory of her arm in Rex Triumph's jaws. "You really don't."

Clay turned his wide eyes to Jade. "But what are you going to do with the Harbinger? You're not going to leave all the dragons asleep, are you?"

"Of course not," Jade said. "But I won't wake them up unless they agree not to cause trouble."

"How can you do that?" Clay asked.

Rose reached out and took Jade's hand.

One thing adults always asked Rose was what she wanted to do with her life. What would she grow up to be? They talked about doing something to change the world—like curing a disease, making a new invention, flying to Mars, or getting elected president. But Rose Gallagher knew she was going to change the world in a way nobody had ever imagined. Together with Jade, they were going to restore a powerful civilization that had disappeared millions of years before. Someday, somehow, they would awaken the dragons again.

"We'll figure it out together," Rose said.

That was not the only gift she had left him. He set the avisaurus down on his desk and picked up the dagger that Rose Gallagher had rammed into his shoulder.

It was a thing of indescribable beauty. The magnificence of the object could only be appreciated in the sunlight, and Jade had shaped it in a hurry, in the dead of night. He held it up to catch the rays of the Nevada sun, watching the golden light ripple and dance across the facets of the diamond surface. The edge was a half-inch strip of smooth crystal as clear as still water, but the rest of the weapon was adorned with intricate patterns of ridges that stretched across the blade like the veins of a leaf. It was an ironic piece of work. Here was the largest diamond on Earth, cut and polished as if by a master gem smith, incalculably valuable...and grafted to a common trowel.

There had been no need to make it so beautiful. He doubted Jade had realized what she was doing when she shaped it with such delicate precision. All that detail had come from somewhere deep in the mind of Rose Gallagher.

Dragons did not make things like this.

It was a human thing, made with the power of a dragon.

Triumph considered that for a long time. He had

Epilogue

Rex Triumph held out his arm. "Come now," he called softly. "Come to me."

A small blue-and-red form fluttered into view. It darted in to land on a banister, wobbling slightly as it found its footing. The creature looked at him with bright, piercing eyes and let out a singsong chirp. Then the avisaurus took flight, swooped across the length of the vast penthouse apartment, and settled to rest on Rex Triumph's arm.

"That's good," he whispered to it.

The little birdlike dinosaur was the only one of his creations that had not turned back into an automaton of plastic and steel. He'd wondered if it was an oversight on the part of the young Archon, but more likely it was a gift.

"Just the sort of tenderhearted thing she would do," he said.

recoiled at the idea of a dragon shackling itself to a human, but he had to admit the results were quite beyond his expectations. Rose and Jade had protected each other from his psychic influence so thoroughly that he had been unable to even silence the human child. And they had made armor and weapons, such wonders that neither could have hoped to create on her own.

When they worked in harmony, Rose and Jade were a force far greater than either acting alone.

He touched his thumb to the edge of the diamond dagger, lightly like the brush of a feather. A bead of blood welled up where the point pierced the skin. Triumph watched the scarlet trickle down his flesh, pondering.

Perhaps he should get a human of his own.

Andrew L. Young

GRAYSON TOWLER

has enjoyed a lifelong fascination with dragons, dinosaurs, magic, and the mysteries of the natural world. In addition to being a storyteller, he has been a marketing copy writer, web designer, substitute teacher, comic artist, and small business owner. He and his wife, Candi, live in a house owned by three relatively benevolent cats in Longmont, Colorado.